Silver James likes walks on the wild side and coffee. Okay. She *loves* coffee. Warning: her muse, Iffy, runs with scissors. A cowgirl at heart, she's also been an army officer's wife and mom and has worked in the legal field, fire service and law enforcement. Now retired from the real world, she lives in Oklahoma and spends her days writing with the assistance of her two Newfoundland dogs, the cat who rules them all and the myriad characters living in her imagination. She loves interacting with readers on her blog, Twitter and Facebook. Find her at www.silverjames.com.

Books by Silver James

Harlequin Desire

Red Dirt Royalty Series

Cowgirls Don't Cry

To my dad, who taught me how to ride and all about cowboy honor, to my family for always believing in me, and to Charles, my editor, for his faith in my abilities, his enthusiasm and his patience.

One

Chance Barron always knew exactly what he wanted. At the moment, he'd set his sights on the attractive blonde sitting at the hotel bar.

The late-March blizzard had shut down Chicago O'Hare Airport, and he wasn't going anywhere in a hurry. The weather service predicted the storm would blow over by morning, and he'd be on the first flight back to Oklahoma City. In the meantime, there was a pretty little gal all alone knocking back martinis like water. She'd twisted her hair up on top of her head and secured it with something that looked like a chopstick. Her face remained angled away from him, but the graceful curve of her jaw and neck had him noticing her profile. The red jacket and black slacks showed fashion flair and, despite the snow, she sported boots with impossible heels.

He studied her like she was evidence in a hotly contested case and debated how to phrase his opening argument. She ordered another martini and when the drink was served, he watched her long fingers play with the plastic pick and all but gulped as her full lips slid over the ripe, green olive stuffed with a cocktail onion. His groin tightened as his mind conjured up sexy images. A one-night stand wouldn't hurt, and he'd certainly be in a better mood to deal with the old man when he got home.

Thoughts of his father, Cyrus Barron, intruded at the

worst possible times. Probably because he was a force of nature. Oil. Land and cattle. Politics and media. Name the pie, and Chance's old man owned most of it. Too bad he was such a jackass. He delighted in setting his spurs in the hides of his sons, and Chance was no exception. He had his own law firm, though the family was a big client. He certainly wasn't in charge of the ranch's breeding program but his father had sent him on a fool's errand looking for a stud colt that didn't exist in the state of Illinois. And now he was stuck in the Windy City during a freak March blizzard.

The waitress approached, an interested smile curling her lips. He declined her offer for a refill and handed her a crisp fifty dollar bill to cover his tab and tip. "Keep the change, hon," he drawled. He slid out of the booth and homed in on the bar—only to realize his quarry had escaped.

"Damn." His muttered curse was lost in the clatter of glasses and hum of conversation as he pushed toward the exit. She couldn't have gone far. He'd find her and argue his case for keeping each other warm tonight.

Cassidy Morgan leaned against the window in the hotel lobby, her cell phone pressed to her ear. Outside, fat cotton balls of snow drifted across her view—like staring into the heart of a giant snow globe. Dizzy and a tad claustrophobic, her equilibrium thrown off both physically and emotionally, she closed her eyes.

"I'm not going to make it in time, am I?" The words spoken quietly into the phone were ripped from the depths of her soul.

"No, darlin'." Baxter "Boots" Thomas didn't believe in sugarcoating things. "The doctors don't know how he's hung on this long."

She heard the muted sounds from the heart and respiration monitors beeping in the silence that followed on the other end of the line. And she recognized both the exhaustion and surrender in the voice of her father's best friend.

"Will you put the phone next to his ear? I know he can't hear me but…" Her throat closed, and she blinked hard to clear her vision. She pictured Boots's actions from the rustling sounds and then she heard his muffled, "Go ahead."

She talked. She reminisced. In the end, her voice broke and she cried. When her mother died of pneumonia, Cassie had been three, so young the emotional pain was lost on her. But this? This hurt far more than she had ever imagined it could. She wanted to be there. Wanted to hold his hand as he passed. He'd always been there for her. And she'd always managed to fail him, the disappointment in his eyes apparent to her every time she'd seen him over the past ten years.

Her father's voice whispered in her ear. "Cowgirls don't cry, baby. Ya gotta pick yourself up and ride."

She blinked against the stinging tears and felt his sharply indrawn breath all the way to her toes. Then silence. He was gone. That quickly. Two blinks of her eyelids, his sharply indrawn breath, and the great bear of a man who'd been her father existed no more.

"You okay, baby girl?" Boots was back on the line.

Cass dashed at her eyes with the back of her hand. Hell no, she wasn't okay. But she had to be. She had to take care of things. Whether she wanted to or not. "I'll be there as soon as possible, Uncle Boots. I'm stuck here until the blizzard lets up. Couldn't even get back to my apartment, so I'm spending the night in a hotel here at O'Hare." Her voice remained steady. She couldn't lose it. Not yet.

"I'll be on the first flight out in the morning. I'll call to give you my arrival time." She cleared the lump forming in her throat. "Will you call the funeral home for me? To pick him up. I… Don't let them cremate him until I get there, Uncle Boots. I…I need to see him. To say goodbye. Okay?"

"Sure, baby girl. I'll take care of it."

"You know where he stashed the good stuff. Go home and toast the stubborn old coot for me."

"Sure thing, sugar. Now get your tail home. We've got work to do."

"I love you, Uncle Boots."

"Love you, too, baby girl."

She tapped the red end call bar on her phone and slipped it into her pocket. *Damn, damn, damn.* How could she absorb the enormity of this event and not let it drive her to her knees? She closed her eyes against the prickle of tears. She didn't cry. Not in public. Hadn't she learned that from her dad? Cowgirls were tough. Well, dammit, she wasn't a cowgirl. Not anymore. Not for a long time. Cass continued to rest her hot forehead against the cool glass.

She'd left the ranch behind ten years ago. With dreams of making her mark, she'd chased life in the big city, where stars in the night sky were outshone by light from skyscraper windows, and the rumble of traffic sounded like far-off thunder.

Ranch life was hard. Early mornings. Late nights. Worrying about the weather—searing heat, freezing cold, too much rain or not enough. Early frosts. Diseases that could wipe out a herd in a heartbeat. Rodeo was even harder. Her dad had loved the rodeo. She had, too, once upon a time when she was a little girl insulated from the reality of it all.

Cass did not want to go home. She didn't want to say goodbye to the man against whom she measured every boyfriend. Even hurting him as she had, and regardless of his disappointment in the choices she made, he had continued to love her. And now her dad was gone.

She squared her shoulders and decided she needed to go to bed, despite the allure of another martini. Or a bottle of whiskey. Not that it would help. Booze wouldn't touch the ache in her heart, wouldn't numb the pain like a shot of Novocain administered to an abscessed tooth. That's what her heart felt like. A deep, throbbing abscess full of decay and vile selfishness. She hadn't been back home for a year. And now it was too late.

She reconsidered getting another drink. Or ordering a bottle from room service. She knew that wasn't the answer. Plus, there were other drawbacks. Fighting the crowd at the airport and dealing with things at home while nursing a hangover just didn't appeal.

Cass turned —and buried her nose in a starched white shirt.

"Easy, darlin'."

The man's large hands gripped her biceps and kept her upright despite the fact her knees had turned to jelly. She tilted her head to look up. Quite a ways up. She took in the chiseled jaw shadowed by dark stubble, eyes the color of amber and dark hair—thick, silky and worn just a little long so that it caressed the man's wide forehead and kissed the collar of his crisp shirt. She swallowed. Hard.

"I'm so sorry. I didn't realize you were standing there." At least she didn't stammer. Two points for her. But she cringed inside at how breathless her voice sounded. It was surprise. That's all. She didn't want or need the complication presented by this sexy man right now.

"S'okay, hon. I didn't mean to scare you."

She backed away from him and shook his hands free. "Scare me?" Her brow quirked as she lifted her chin. "I don't scare, mister." Now that she had a good look at him, her brows narrowed in speculation. "You look sort of familiar. Have we met before?"

Cass managed not to blush as those wolf-like eyes traveled over her body from head to toe and back again. A smile she could only describe as appreciative spread across his full lips.

"Honey, as beautiful as you are, I'm sure I'd remember." He held out his hand as if to introduce himself but was interrupted when the theme song from the old television show *Rawhide* emanated from his pocket, startling them both.

A look of anger flashed across his face, and he muttered something that sounded like, "Dammit, I'm busy."

Busy? She stepped back, putting more space between them. For an insane moment, she wondered if he was stalking her. She'd noticed a man in the bar watching her. This guy fit the general description even though the corners of the place were dark, and he'd remained in the shadows.

He fitted a smile on his face but was interrupted again. This time his phone erupted with the sounds of a siren. People stopped, turned and stared. She stepped back farther.

"That sounds like an emergency," she hinted.

Chance fumbled in his jacket pocket and found the blasted phone. He planned to cheerfully kill whichever brother had reprogrammed his ring tones. Stabbing at the screen, he growled, "What!" He held up an index finger to indicate it would be a short conversation, hoping she'd stay.

"Did I catch you at a bad time?"

Chance could feel his brother's smirk through the phone. "It's always a bad time when you call, Cord. Tell the old man not even he can control the weather. I'm stuck in Chicago until this freaking blizzard blows over."

Chance barely listened, his attention focused on the blonde. Something in her expression captured his interest. Every time she blinked, her lashes appeared to leave bruises under her eyes. He peered closer and noticed the dark circles marring the delicate skin. Sadness. That's what he saw on her face and in her eyes.

"Chancellor! Are you even listening to me?"

"No." Not even the use of his full name could distract him.

"Well, you better. He called a family meeting for tomorrow. Clay is flying in from Washington. The old man tried to send one of the planes for you, but every pilot on staff refused to fly because of the weather. Pissed him off to no end, but he couldn't fire all of them."

Chance resisted the urge to scrub at his forehead. The old man's temper and propensity for firing people kept Chance hip deep in fixing the messes made by his father. In fact, he cleaned up all the predicaments his family got embroiled in. It was his duty, according to Cyrus Barron, and part of the price to pay for being a member of one of Oklahoma's richest and most powerful families. The perks of being a Barron were many, so Chance paid the dues.

"I have a seat on the first flight out in the morning. Any clue about the hornet's nest we're walking into?"

"Trouble with a capital T. The old man's worn a path in the carpet from all his pacing. He keeps muttering something about 'that old bastard thinks he can outsmart me by dying' with a lot more choice cuss words sprinkled liberally throughout. He had a map spread out on the conference table, so I have the feeling he's in acquisition mode and isn't going to take no for an answer."

"So what else is new?" The rhetorical nature of the question was lost on Cord. Chance resisted the urge to hang up on his brother as he continued to watch the girl. He liked her looks, but the playboy side of his brain told him to run. The abiding sorrow in her eyes boded nothing but trouble—and entanglements. With his father on the warpath, he couldn't afford either one. He tuned back in to his brother's voice.

"It's not enough that Clay is a senator. The old man is bugging Chase to run for governor next year."

This was a conversation he didn't want a stranger to overhear. He turned his back and stepped a few feet away. "Chase? In politics? Oh hell, no. Trouble follows him like an ambulance-chasing lawyer. The old man must be losing his grip on reality."

"Hey, at least he's not after you or me, bro."

Chance snorted. "I had that conversation with the old man when I was twelve."

Cord laughed again, harder this time. "Yeah, I remember that. You couldn't sit a saddle for almost a week after he finished tanning your hide with that switch. And he got back at you by making you go to law school."

Chance turned around just in time to see his plans evaporate behind the elevator doors. He laughed as he saw the woman lean over to continue watching him until the doors closed. His intellect remained curious about her. His body had a more basic interest involving naked skin and sheets. He could still smell the scent of her perfume, or shampoo or simply her. Almonds, orange and a hint of cinnamon—the fragrance as distinctive as the woman. With a frustrated snarl, he focused on his brother's voice yammering in his ear.

"The old man is livid, Chance. I've never seen him like this. Not even when Tammy ran off with the foreman. I'm worried he's actually going to stroke out."

Chance rolled his eyes. Tammy was wife number six. Or seven. Half his father's age and built like Dolly Parton, she'd turned her charms on the ranch foreman and convinced him to take off with her. The Barrons owned the two major papers in Oklahoma so she'd threatened to go to the tabloids with fabricated family secrets. She would sink to that level to cause a scandal. As the family lawyer, Chance negotiated a monetary settlement to avoid the nuisance and filed the divorce papers while the ink was still wet on her signature.

"So what the hell's going on, Cord? You just cost me a roll in the hay. There'd better be a damn good reason for the old man's fit."

"Does the name Ben Morgan mean anything to you?"

Chance rifled through his memory. "Vaguely. Old rodeo cowboy, right?"

"That's him. The old man and Morgan butted heads a few times, including once over a woman."

"Aw, hell… Which one of the stepmonsters?"

"That's the funny thing. None of them. This was years ago. Before he married Mom."

Chance rubbed his forehead. "Damn, Cord. I know the old man is legendary for holding a grudge, but that's a little ridiculous."

"You're telling me? I'm the one he's been cussing the last few minutes, ever since he found out Morgan died tonight." Cord paused for a breath. "He's upset enough he forgot about your failure to find the colt."

"Now you're giving me grief about that, too? Come on."

"Hey, you know how he reacts to losing, little brother. The good news, he's distracted. There's some sort of legal BS involving this Ben Morgan guy. The old man wants you to wade through it. Thought I'd give you a heads-up so you don't walk in blind."

"Thanks for the warning. I'll fire up the laptop and do some research."

"I'll email the particulars. And Chance? Sorry if I messed up any sort of extracurricular activity you might have planned for later."

"Yeah, right. I can hear the remorse ringing in your voice. I'll head to the office straight from the airport when I get back tomorrow."

"I'll let you know if anything changes."

Chance tapped his phone and dropped it into his pocket. This whole trip had gone to hell in a handbasket, and now he was quoting the old man's clichés. That was so not a good sign. He glanced toward the bar. The waitress would get off sooner or later but after getting up close and personal with the blonde, his desire for any other woman waned—at least for tonight. In three strides, he reached the elevator and stabbed the button. He had work to do.

Two

Cass loosened her seat belt as the flight attendant announced the flight would be delayed. Seemed a passenger was running late. The economy section was packed, so it had to be somebody in first class. She rolled her head on her neck and listened as her vertebrae snapped, crackled and popped. Better to sound like a bowlful of Rice Krispies than suffer the headache that would follow.

She closed her eyes and tried to forget her situation. Going home was always hard—that's why she'd avoided it for so long, even though Boots had urged her to visit. And now with her dad gone—with things left unsaid and apologies not made, her heart hurt. She swallowed her guilt but it churned in her stomach like raw jalapeños. Cass forced her thoughts away from her dad. She'd say goodbye when she got to the funeral home, but until then, she'd just have to hope he had heard what was in her heart when she talked to him last night.

The pilot's voice echoed over the intercom, scratchy and hard to hear over the hum of conversations. Evidently, whoever they'd been waiting for had arrived, and they were finally ready for takeoff. She braced her feet against the floor and clasped her hands in her lap. Flying was not her favorite activity, especially getting off the ground and landing. She measured her breathing, concentrating on remaining calm, then remembered the scent of the guy in the hotel.

Leather and rain on a hot day. That's what he smelled like—an odd combination that evoked memories of her childhood growing up on the ranch and around rodeo arenas all over the West.

He'd been wearing a starched white shirt with a button-down collar, like a banker, but it was tucked into a pair of well-fitting jeans, even if they were pressed to a knife-edged crease. Her brow furrowed. He'd also been wearing boots. Not that people in Chicago didn't wear Western boots. Some of them even wore them "for real," not just as a fashion statement.

Her stomach dropped away as the plane rumbled into the cloudy skies, chasing all thoughts of the guy out of her head. The fuselage shuddered several times before she heard grinding as the landing gear retracted. The plane continued to climb at a steep incline, and the pilot mumbled something about weather and flying altitude that she couldn't really hear over the throbbing in her ears. She swallowed to make her eardrums pop, pushed back against her seat and returned to thinking about her close encounter.

Had the timing been different, she might have let the guy buy her a drink, just to see what percolated between them. He was sexy as all get-out. Tall. Muscular. His hands strong as they gripped her arms, but with a certain amount of gentleness. She wasn't petite by any measure, but he'd towered over her. He radiated heat, too, or maybe he just touched something in her that created heat. She hadn't been so intrigued by a man in ages. Then she remembered the reason for her trip, and all thoughts of the sexy encounter fled.

I'm sorry, Daddy. She offered the apology to the heavens, knowing it covered so much more than her wayward thoughts. Cass squiggled her nose, fighting the burn of tears. She couldn't cry. Not here. Not now.

Her dad's voice echoed softly in her memory, reminding her to be strong. She flashed back to the time she'd just lost the final round of a barrel-racing event by mere tenths of a second. That she'd lost to the reigning national champion, who was twenty years older didn't mean a thing. At the age of seven, all she'd wanted was that shiny buckle and the saddle that went with it for winning.

"No, Daddy. No time for tears. Cowgirls just get back on and ride." Back in the present, she whispered the words in the hopes that saying them out loud would make them true. She hadn't been a cowgirl for ten years. Not since she'd left home to attend college back East. Not since she'd taken the job in Chicago. In fact, she'd only been on a horse a handful of times since then. She hated going home. Hated the heat and dust, the smell of cattle manure.

She didn't want to be a cowgirl. She'd liquidate the ranch, get Boots set up somewhere comfortable and haul ass back to Chicago where she belonged. No regrets. It's what her dad would expect her to do. She'd told him often enough she'd never be back, never take over the ranch.

Those guilty jalapeños boiled and raged in her stomach again. Returning to Chicago was the right thing. Really. She conjured up the picture of her close encounter from the night before in her mind, shutting out the remorse. His chiseled face still seemed familiar, and she felt as if she should know him. Was he an actor? Or maybe a professional cowboy? She nudged the feeling this way and that, seeking an answer, but didn't find one.

The passenger in front of her shoved his seat all the way back jostling her tray table so that the coffee, served moments before by the flight attendant, sloshed out. The man on her right in the window seat snored as his head fell over toward her shoulder. She dodged him but bumped the woman on her left. That earned her a scathing look. Cass rolled her eyes and shrugged. She could only hope this flight from hell ended sooner rather than later.

She gulped what little coffee didn't spill and passed off

the sodden napkin and cup to the attendant as she came back down the aisle. Feeling far too much like a sardine for comfort, Cass closed her eyes and tried to sleep. Thoughts of the handsome cowboy danced in her head. She was positive she knew him from somewhere. Since she didn't watch much TV, she discarded the idea he might be an actor. Could he be someone she'd met in college? Or, heaven forbid, high school? She didn't have the best memory for faces, but there was just something about the man.

Giving up any pretense of relaxation, she shoved her tray table up and fastened it with the little lever, using a lot more force than technically necessary. Then she stretched her legs under the seat in front of her and drummed her toes against the bottom of it. When the occupant twisted to stare at her over the top of the reclined seatback, she flashed the smile of a two-year-old brat. And didn't care. The man eventually turned around and since he raised the seat a few inches, she quit kicking.

More memories of her dad swamped her. Moisture filled her eyes, and her nose stung. She blinked rapidly and had to sort through more guilt. She was a terrible daughter. Her dad had died, and she couldn't be bothered to get there in time to say goodbye. If she never saw the ranch again, never saw Oklahoma again, it would suit her just fine. Yes, she was selfish. She admitted it. So there. Boots had begged her for months to come, and she'd stalled. Her dad had been too proud to call. And she'd been too proud to bend. Now it was too late.

When the tears finally came, Cass dashed them from her eyes with the back of her hand. Her elbow caught the arm of the passenger sitting on her left. The woman exhaled, the sound uncompromisingly disdainful as she shifted away from the contact. The guy on her right just snored, mouth open and drool threatening Cassie's wool blazer.

Already walking a fine line between anger and grief,

Cass lost control. "Well, pardon my tears." She didn't bother
to keep her voice down. "My father died last night, and
I was stuck in a freakin' blizzard and didn't get there in
time. I'm on my way home to bury him. If my crying is
too much of an imposition, you can just move your...self
to another seat."

Around her, the hum of conversation petered off into
silence. She could tell from the heat radiating off her face
that she'd turned beet-red—a legacy from her mother. She
flushed scarlet whenever she got mad, cried or laughed too
hard. Yeah, that was Cassidy Morgan. She wasn't pretty
when her emotions ruled. Unfortunately, that was a great
deal of the time. At the moment, her emotions slammed
her with a double whammy.

The woman stared, mouth gaping, left speechless by
Cassie's outburst.

Cassie bit back any further retort, instead, settling back
into her seat. She crossed her arms over her chest and stared
stone-faced straight ahead, ignoring everyone.

Chance sipped his French roast coffee from a ceramic
mug and skimmed the information on his laptop screen.
He was learning all sorts of interesting things about his
father he couldn't wait to share with his brothers. To hear
the old man tell it now, he'd been born with a gold spoon
up his... Chance reined in that thought and tried to scrub
the image from his brain.

But back when Chance's mother was still alive, the old
man had been all about hard work and scrabbling to put the
Barron name on the map. Chance's research from the night
before showed Cyrus had worked the oil patch, ranched and
even been a rodeo rider on the side.

And he'd loved a woman named Colleen before he'd met
and married Chance's mother, Alice. According to the papers at the time, Cyrus Barron had done a stint in county

jail after a spectacular fight at a rodeo in Fort Worth. He'd put Ben Morgan in the hospital and ended the man's promising bronc-riding career. Colleen had turned her back on Cyrus and married Ben within weeks. Oh, yeah. The old man didn't hold a grudge; he got even. He'd been dogging Ben Morgan's steps ever since, throwing up roadblocks in an attempt to grind the other man beneath his boot heel. But Ben Morgan didn't have any "give up" in him. He'd made a life for his wife, first as a supplier of rodeo stock then as a horse trainer.

Chance rubbed the back of his neck. His father was a royal jerk. He couldn't even let the man have peace in the grave. The email from Cord first thing this morning had confirmed that Morgan had taken out a loan at a small bank—the bank recently purchased by a subsidiary of Barron Enterprises, and he'd used the ranch as collateral. The old man wanted Chance to stop off and pick up the file before coming into the office. Since he could no longer screw with Ben Morgan, Cyrus planned to screw with any heirs or successors his old nemesis might have by calling the note.

Yeah, leave it to his father to be four moves ahead of any opponent. Chance had to admire the old man's business acumen. He'd thought the acquisition foolish at the time and certainly not worth the hassle of the federal and state banking regulators' paperwork. Chance had hired a couple of experts in banking law to handle it because Cyrus had remained adamant. The old man wanted the bank. So they'd bought it. Chance knew why now. He tossed off a mental shrug. Barron Enterprises could afford it.

Closing the laptop, he held up his mug for a refill as the flight attendant hovered, a ready smile on her face.

"You know, I have layovers in OKC sometimes," she whispered. She wrapped one hand around his to steady the cup as she poured, a move he recognized as an excuse to touch him.

Chance glanced up. She was a brunette, in her late twenties, and her trim uniform fit in all the right places. The girl was just his type—female—but even as he smiled, another face appeared in his memory. The blonde from the hotel. His abdomen contracted, and his heart thundered for a few beats. He hadn't even gotten her name, yet here she was haunting him.

"Sorry, hon. This is just a quick trip for me." The lie flowed smooth as honey from his mouth. As disappointment registered on her face, Chance wondered what the hell had gotten into him. Why would he turn down a sure thing?

While it was unlikely he'd ever cross paths with the woman, he did have a brother who was a private investigator and ran Barron Security. He'd sic Cash on her trail. All Chance wanted was one night to get her out of his system. That's all it would take.

He shifted in his seat, glad the tray table and computer disguised his discomfort. He couldn't pinpoint why the woman had gotten under his skin but she had, like a burr under his saddle. He shoved thoughts of her away and opened his laptop again, hoping to concentrate on the task at hand. He had to squelch his libido and his uneasiness over what his father wanted—the combination made for an odd sensation in and of itself.

The flight attendant scurried toward the economy section. He leaned into the aisle to see what was happening. Three attendants hovered around a row of seats toward the back of the plane. Everyone with aisle seats had twisted to watch the commotion, too. He heard raised voices, but the conversation was too indistinct. Within moments, the situation calmed. He returned his attention to the problem at hand.

Once the plane landed, he was the first one off. With no luggage to retrieve, he headed straight for the parking lot. He stepped into the gentle March sunshine, glad he hadn't bothered to shrug into his heavy winter jacket. The storm pounding the upper Midwest hadn't dipped as far south as Oklahoma, and Chance was thankful. He hated cold weather. Of course, he hated hot weather, too. If he had his way, he'd live somewhere where the temperature remained at a balmy sixty-eight degrees year-round.

He dug out his car keys, hit the button for the auto-unlock and dumped his carry-on suitcase and laptop case in the passenger seat before settling behind the wheel. With a reckless abandon born from experience, Chance maneuvered his sleek, phantom-black Audi R8 sports car toward the parking lot exit. The car swooped down the exit ramp, slowing to a stop just long enough for him to pay the attendant.

Without looking for merging traffic from other lanes, he downshifted and gunned the powerful 571 horsepower V10 engine. A flash of rust in the corner of his eye and the sound of squealing tires had him handling the powerful vehicle like a race car to avoid a collision. Caught by the next traffic light, Chance glanced over at the beat-up old pickup in the next lane. He looked away then looked back. He didn't recognize the old man in the driver's seat but the passenger? Oh, yeah. It was her! The blonde from the hotel. She'd rolled down the window, and her glare could melt the metallic paint right off the Audi.

His windows were tinted dark, and he doubted she could see him. When the light changed, instead of accelerating the way he normally would, he eased off the clutch, making sure the clunker pulled ahead of him. He made a mental note of the license plate. Now he'd have a chance to sic Cash on her and move in for the kill after all. He grinned, unable to calculate the odds of seeing her again, especially here on his home ground. Excitement tingled in his fingertips. Life was looking up. Gunning his engine, he headed toward I-40 and the command performance he had to attend.

Three

"Did you see that idiot? He could have killed us!"

"City folks drive a bit faster, sugar. That's all. We didn't wreck." Boots turned his head and spit out the window.

"You shouldn't chew, Uncle Boots. That stuff's bad for you."

"It's the only vice I got left, Cassie, and I ain't gonna live forever. Give an old man some peace."

She ground her back teeth together but held her tongue. The seat cover—an old horse blanket—made her back itch through her cotton turtleneck. She'd shed her heavy jacket as soon as she'd stepped out of the terminal. Compared to Chicago, the fifty degree temperature in Oklahoma City felt positively balmy. The Australian shepherd sprawled on the bench seat between them yawned, and she absently scratched his ears.

"I want your life, Buddy. Nothing to do all day but nap in the sun and chase squirrels. And you don't have to put up with the stupid people of the world. You can just bite 'em or piss on 'em."

"You watch your mouth, Cassidy Anne Morgan. I won't have you corrupting this poor dog with such language. Ol' Buddy here is sensitive."

She rolled her eyes but reached over to pat Boots on the shoulder. "Yessir."

They rode in silence for several minutes. The old man

cleared his throat but didn't speak. A few blocks later, caught by another red light, he glanced at Cassie. "I'm gonna miss him, sugar." Buddy whined softly and shifted to lay his head on the man's thigh, as if to say he'd miss Ben, too.

Cass pressed her lips together and lost the battle with her tears. They streaked her cheeks even as Boots pulled a faded red bandanna from his pocket and offered it to her. She took it and dabbed at her runny nose, but the tears continued. She leaned her head against the window.

"Why didn't you tell me?"

"Tell you what, Cassie? I asked you to come home lots of times."

"You could have told me he was dying."

"I told you he was sick."

Her temper flared. "There's a big damn difference between sick and dying, Boots!" Her tears stopped as her anger surged.

"And there's a big damn difference between being too stubborn to come home and make amends and being too busy to worry about your daddy."

"He started it." She winced. That sounded so petulant. But it was true. Her dad had fought her plans the whole way. If she had to go to college, why wasn't one of the local universities good enough? Why did she have to go traipsing off where he'd never get to see her? She'd saved her barrel-racing money and made straight As to get an academic scholarship. Even so, she'd had to wait tables to make ends meet while in college. Then she got a job with the Chicago Mercantile Exchange. Granted, she was far from rich, but she didn't have to haul her butt out of bed at the crack of dawn to do barn chores. She didn't have to muck the manure out of stalls or round up cattle too stupid to seek shelter in a storm.

Boots made a choking noise so she glanced over at him.

His face shone with tears and his white-knuckled grip on the steering wheel indicated how upset he was. She leaned over the dog and placed her hand on his.

"You're right, Uncle Boots."

"Aw, honey. The two of you are so dang much alike. Stubborn to the core. But he loved you. And he was proud of you."

"No." She shook her head, unable to believe that. "No, he wasn't. I disappointed him. I didn't stay here to help with the ranch. I didn't get married and give him grandbabies. I didn't do anything with my life that he wanted me to do."

"All he ever wanted was for you to be happy, baby girl."

Cass didn't know what to say. She knew in her heart Boots was wrong. She'd disappointed her dad from the day she'd turned eighteen, lost her virginity in the back of a pickup at the National Western Stock Show and Rodeo in Denver and decided she'd never get on a horse again.

The old truck rattled across a speed bump as Boots turned it into the parking lot at the funeral home. He pulled into a parking space and shoved the transmission into Park. Neither of them moved. She did not want to get out and walk inside that building. With its white-washed stucco and blue shutters topped by a red-tiled roof, the place looked more like a Mexican restaurant than a funeral home. Part of her wanted to ask Boots to just drive away. The other part knew that if she turned tail and ran she'd regret it for the rest of her life.

Cass sucked in a deep breath and held it. Letting the air hiss out slowly, she wiped her face and nose with the bandanna then stuck it in her pocket, just in case. "Okay. Let's get this over with."

The doors on the old truck creaked as they opened. Buddy jumped out after Boots, and he scolded the dog.

"Leave him be, Uncle Boots. He has as much right to say

goodbye to Daddy as anyone." She met him on the sidewalk and slipped her arm through his. "We can do this. Right?"

Boots patted her hand where it rested on his forearm. "You know what your daddy always said, sugar."

"Yeah. Often and loudly." She inhaled deeply again. "Cowgirls don't cry, they just get back on and ride. I really hate that phrase, you know."

He chuckled and gave her hand another pat.

Boots distracted the officious man who met them at the door while Cassie snuck past, Buddy at her heels. They were probably breaking some law but she didn't care. Buddy needed this goodbye as much as she did.

Alone in a private viewing room a few minutes later, Cass stared at what used to be her father. A sheet covered his body from shoulders to toes. There'd be no burying clothes or makeup on his face since he'd be cremated once she left. The funeral home had kept the body solely for her chance to say goodbye.

His face had thinned with the years, as had his hair. And the crinkles around his eyes looked like they'd been etched in wax. This…thing wasn't her father. He'd been full of life. Of laughter. And a few choice cuss words. She reached out as if to touch his hand but couldn't follow through. The cancer had stolen his vitality. The thought of her skin touching that cold facsimile of her dad made her stomach roil.

"Oh, Daddy." The words clogged up her throat as sorrow surged. "God, I miss you. I'm so sorry. I'm so sorry for everything. Please forgive me?" She closed her eyes against the salty sting, and her throat ached from swallowing her sobs. With her arms pressed across her stomach, she swayed with the rhythm of her grief. Something warm leaned against her leg, and Buddy's whine joined her choking sobs. She dropped one hand to rest on the dog's head, her fingers burrowing into the soft fur. "You miss him, too, Buddy. I know. What the hell are we going to do now?"

* * *

Chance sat in the bank's parking lot making notes as he talked to Cash on the phone. "So Ben Morgan has a daughter." An heir complicated matters, but he could file enough paperwork to keep the estate tied up until he could get the loan called. Morgan had been desperate so there was a balloon payment—due and owing on a date certain. "Do you have a name?"

"Cassidy. I've put a tracer on her. Oh, and speaking of, I have the information you wanted on that tag. Truck belongs to a guy named Baxter Thomas."

A memory nudged him again. "Where do I know that name from?"

"Ya got me, Chance. Want me to run his financials?"

"No. Just do a quick Google search. See what comes up." He drummed his fingers on the leather-clad steering wheel as he listened to clicking keys through the cell phone.

His brother's low whistle caught his attention. "Now that's interesting. Baxter Thomas is also Boots Thomas."

"The rodeo clown?" They weren't called that anymore—now they were called bullfighters, which was more appropriate to what they did inside the arena. Boots Thomas was a legend and anyone who'd ever traveled the rodeo circuit knew his name.

"That's the one. And according to this article, he and Ben Morgan were partners in a rodeo stock company." Cash whistled again. "And the plot thickens. Cassidy Morgan was a champion cowgirl back in the day, but she quit after winning the Denver Stock Show ten years ago. That's the year you and Cord won the team roping up there."

"Well, damn." Had he met her on the rodeo circuit? He couldn't put a face with the name so probably not. His rodeo career pretty much ended after that night. He graduated from college that spring and started law school soon after. He didn't have time to chase steers or cowgirls.

"Chance? Are you listening?"

He wasn't. "What?"

"There's a memorial service for Morgan day after tomorrow at the Pleasant Hills Funeral Home. As near as I can figure, it's a cremation. I suppose it'd be really uncool to serve her with the papers at the service."

"Ya think? Jeez, Cash, you've been hanging around the old man too long. What time is the memorial?"

"Ten in the morning. Why? You aren't thinking about actually showing up, are you?"

He didn't examine his motives very closely as he answered. "It might be a good idea to go. Just to get a feel for things." Business. This was just business. But he could do business without being a jerk—even if his father wanted to steal a ranch out from under his enemy's grieving daughter. He didn't believe in coincidences, but the odds of his mystery girl being Cassidy Morgan just kept getting better.

Armed with the information he needed, Chance started his car and headed home. He had plenty of time to get the legal papers filed. First, he wanted a shower and a change of clothes because he felt slimy all of a sudden. Like a royal SOB. He had plenty of time to get the legal papers filed.

He was about to act the world's biggest bully, all under the orders of the bastard who sired him. At a stoplight, he glanced at his reflection in the rearview mirror. "You are a complete slimeball, you know that, right?" He didn't blink at the accusation. He always told the truth, at least to himself.

Lost in thought, the light turned green, but he didn't notice until someone honked. He waved a hand hoping the car behind saw the gesture as an apology, and wondered why the hell that mattered. He was a Barron. If he wanted to sit through a whole light, he would. He accelerated through the intersection and put his thoughts on hold until he arrived at his condo. Thinking about stealing the ranch from Cassidy

Morgan would only make things worse. He barked a wry laugh. As if. He wasn't sure how they could get any worse.

Cassie wore black—suit jacket, matching skirt and heels—and felt out of place. Colorful Western clothes abounded, the room resembling a patchwork quilt—homey and warm, like the people who wore them. The small chapel was bursting at the seams with an array of folks—old rodeo hands, neighbors, the friends garnered from a lifetime of living. Death was just another part of all that living. Her dad once commented that suits were for marryin' and buryin', but nobody said they had to be black. She should have remembered that.

The front of the room looked like a field of wildflowers. No fussy formal arrangements. She didn't know the minister, but he seemed to know all about her dad. While short, his eulogy painted a vivid picture of the man. When he finished, he invited any who wished to share a few words or a memory.

Near the back, a man cleared his throat. Chairs scraped and creaked on the wooden floor, followed by the sound of heavy boots marching up the aisle. A big bear of a man, with a scraggly beard, a paunch overhanging the huge rodeo buckle on his belt and a chaw of tobacco in his cheek stepped forward.

"Ben Morgan saved my life some forty years ago. We were dang sure dumb back in our twenties. At the Fort Worth rodeo, I got hung up on a bull named Red Devil. Ol' Boots here was working the arena as a clown, and Ben rode the pickup horse. While Boots kept Devil occupied, Ben jumped off his horse, grabbed that bull by the ear and rode him down to his knees so the other boys could cut me free. Next thing I knew, I'm sitting on my ass in the dirt, and Ben is flyin' across the arena. That dang bull broke three of Ben's ribs but he got right up, dusted off his britches and went on with his job. He was a helluva man, and he'll be missed."

A chorus of yesses and amens followed the man back down the aisle. A woman approached the microphone next. She paused to offer her hand to Cassie and gave Boots's shoulder a pat. At the lectern, she turned a 100-watt smile on the congregation. "Most of y'all know me. For those who don't, I'm Nadine Jackson, and I own the Four Corners Diner. Ben came in most every day before he got sick. But all the regulars kept up with him through Boots. Ben'd give you the shirt off his back if you needed it. He didn't have deep pockets, but if a cowboy was down on his luck, Ben always had a few bucks to spare and dinner to share. My granddaughter called him the Louis L'Amour Cowboy."

She paused to let the chuckles from the crowd die down. "She's only eight, so I'm pleased the little darlin' even knows who Mr. L'Amour is. But she's right. Ben could've been a hero in one of those books. He was tall, rugged and believed in doin' the right thing no matter what. He was the kind of man a body would be proud to call friend."

Nadine turned her smile toward Cassie. "And you, honey? You was his pride and joy. He couldn't stop talkin' about you. Your buckles and trophies from back when you were a champion cowgirl, your report cards and your college graduation. 'My little girl is a college graduate, Nadine,' he told me. 'She's made somethin' of herself.'"

Cassie's ribs seemed to constrict around her lungs, and she couldn't breathe. Pain. There was so much pain in her heart. She gripped her hands together until her knuckles turned white. Tears prickled behind her eyelids, and she swallowed around the lump clogging her throat. *Oh, Daddy, I'm so sorry.* She sent the prayer winging into the cosmos, hoping her father would catch a whisper of it.

"I just have one more thing to say," Nadine continued. "The Four Corners is closed to the public today. I figure poor Cassie ain't in any shape to be hosting this herd at home, so I'm throwin' open the doors. Y'all come on by, grab a bite t'eat and reminisce some about Ben."

When no one else came forward, the minister speared Cassie with a long look. She sat for a moment to gather her thoughts and steel her emotions. Boots gave her clenched hands a little squeeze. She leaned over, kissed his cheek and stood. From the podium, she gazed out over the room and was struck once more by the bright colors and the kind, honest faces of her father's friends. They knew him so much better than she. He wouldn't want her wearing black on this day, wouldn't want her tears or her remorse.

Movement in the doorway caught her attention, and her breath froze for a moment when she thought she recognized the figure ducking out. Impossible. There was no way that man could have been the same one at the hotel in Chicago. The hair prickled on the back of her neck and she got a shivery feeling. Her dad would have said someone was walking across her grave. She shivered again, doing her best to ignore the premonition.

"Daddy…" Her voice broke, and she coughed to clear the frog in her throat. Feeling a bit stronger now, she tried again. "Daddy was full of sayings, most of them taken from Louis L'Amour books." She offered Nadine a tentative smile. "We have a whole wall of them at the house, and I grew up on their truisms. Dad also had a tendency to tell me, 'Shoulda, coulda, woulda, honey, just opens the door to regrets. That's the worst thing a person can do—live a life full of regrets.'"

She bit her lip and stared out the door where that mysterious figure seemed to be waiting in the shadows. "I should have been a better daughter. And I could have. Would I if circumstances had been different? I don't know. But I do believe Daddy wouldn't want me worrying about the past. He lived and loved life to the absolute fullest. We can honor him best by doing the same." She glanced over at Boots and was puzzled by the look on his face. Something was going on, something he didn't want to tell her. She'd pin him down soon.

"Thank you all for coming, for being my dad's friends. And thank you, Nadine, for your gracious offer of Four Corners. I never did learn to cook." She glanced down at the speckled gray-and-black box that held her father's ashes. "Hard to believe that a man bigger than life can be reduced to a little box like that. What's left of his body might be in there, but his spirit is riding free. Nothing could ever contain it. Not a hardscrabble life and certainly not death."

Cass stepped away from the microphone and was immediately enveloped in a big hug from Boots. Within moments, they were surrounded by well-wishers, despite her resolve to get to the lobby area to see if her imagination was playing tricks on her. The hairs on her neck rose again, and she could have sworn someone was staring at her. As surreptitiously as she could, she scanned the room, but no one triggered the sense of her being…hunted. She shivered.

"I need to get outside, Uncle Boots." She breathed the words out in a rush and added a few "I'm sorry, excuse me's" in her wake. Stepping into the balmy temperature of the early spring morning didn't quell the feeling of being stalked.

A man wearing a black Stetson caught her eye. He strode across the parking lot headed toward a massive Ford pickup. Broad shoulders tapered to a really fine pair of jeans— could it be the guy from Chicago? That wasn't possible. No way, no how. The shiver dancing through her this time had nothing to do with fear.

Chance escaped before she recognized him. Traffic wasn't heavy enough to curtail his thoughts, which left him wanting nothing more than a tall scotch and a cold shower. What in the world had possessed him to attend the memorial service? Who was he trying to kid? Cassidy Morgan. He was drawn to her like a honeybee to clover. Crossing paths with her in Chicago had been a fluke but now he knew where to find her.

Her face as she eulogized her father was far too reminiscent of her expression in the hotel lobby. He'd probably bumped into her right after she received the news about her father's passing. Chance didn't do vulnerable but this woman had an inner spark that drew him like a bull to a red cape. He wanted her, plain and simple—even if there was nothing simple about this situation.

His cell phone rang, and he punched the button on the steering wheel for the Bluetooth connection. He snarled into the hidden microphone, "What?"

"Dang, bro. Don't be biting my head off."

"What do you want, Cord?"

"Cash and I tracked down that stud colt the old man wanted. You're not going to believe where he is."

"Dammit. Does he want me chasing a horse or stealing a ranch out from under a woman who just buried her father?"

"Whoa, dude. Back up there a minute. That almost sounded like you've developed a conscience."

Chance rubbed his temple and gave up trying to talk and drive at the same time. He pulled off and realized he'd parked a block from the Four Corners. How the hell had that happened? He jammed the transmission into Park and leaned his head back against the headrest on the driver's seat. "Okay, Cord, so tell me where the damn horse is."

"Right here. The plot thickens, little brother. Ben Morgan bought that colt months before you headed north to track him down. He's been under our noses all along."

He sat up straighter. "The ranch and everything on it is collateral. The colt, too?"

"No clue, but Cash is pulling financials. I'll keep you

posted. In the meantime, the old man wants to accelerate things. Can you call the balloon payment immediately?"

"Our father is a real SOB, Cord."

His brother's ringing laughter filled the cab. "So what else is new?" Cord broke the connection before Chance could retort anything.

He stared out the windshield. "So what's that make us, big brother?"

Four

The screen door banged shut behind her. The room hadn't changed one iota in her entire life. She stopped short as countless memories washed over her.

Don't run in the house.

Don't slam the door.

No, you can't bring that baby skunk inside.

Boots sprawled in the worn wooden chair on the porch, Buddy at his feet. A small metal table separated his chair from its twin. Her father's chair. How many evenings had she worked on her homework at the kitchen table, listening to the two men talk through the open window? She passed off an icy glass of sweet tea to Boots then grabbed a third chair, a refugee from some 1950s patio set, and settled into it.

"What are you not sayin', Cassie?"

She'd put off this discussion for almost a week. So much for easing into the conversation. There was no way to soften her news, so she blurted it out. "I'm putting the ranch up for sale." When Boots didn't respond, she plunged ahead. "I don't need the money. Not really. I want to set you up with a little place closer to town. A place where you and Buddy and a horse and some cows can live and be happy."

She gulped down a breath and continued. "It's for the best, you know. I have a life in Chicago. A job. Friends. I left the ranch and never intended to come back, and I wouldn't know what to do with it and…and…" Her voice trailed off as she raised her gaze to meet his. "Say something, Uncle Boots. Don't just sit there staring at me like I've grown a second head."

"You can't sell the ranch."

"Yes, I can. It's mine." She snapped her mouth shut. Maybe it wasn't hers. Maybe her father had left the place to Boots. "Isn't it?"

"Sort of."

"What's that mean?"

"You're Ben's heir, but the place is in hock to the bankers."

"What did Daddy do, Uncle Boots?"

"He took out a loan, Cassie, to pay the medical bills. The note on the land is coming due soon."

She winced, shut her eyes and rubbed at her temples. "How much?"

"A bunch."

"Define a bunch, Uncle Boots." Money. This she understood.

"More than what your daddy has in the bank. More than what I have in the bank. And unless you've made a fortune I don't know about, more than what you have."

"What was he thinking?" The words burst from her mouth before she could stop them.

"He was thinking about paying his bills."

The censure in Boots's tone burned, but she deserved it. "I didn't mean that the way it sounded. But if Dad took out a loan, he must have had a plan. He didn't believe in being in debt." She tried to feel hopeful while waiting for that proverbial other shoe to drop.

"Cattle."

"Cattle?"

"Before he was diagnosed, he bought a herd of five hundred feeder calves cheap. Had them on grass all winter so they're fat and almost ready for market. Give 'em another few weeks, and they'll bring top price. Grass-fed beef is the big thing now, so those calves should make enough to pay off the balloon payment with plenty to cover the rest of his debts to the hospital and leave you a little start-up cash."

"Start-up cash? Did he really believe I'd come back here to stay? With him gone? Why would I do that?" She gulped and quickly added, "Not that I don't love you, Uncle Boots."

"You need to come with me." He heaved up out of his chair.

He limped going down the steps, Buddy close on his heels, and she remembered Boots was even older than her father. He had to be pushing seventy. Man and dog ambled toward the barn and a few moments later, Cass followed. She caught up and as they entered the dim environs of the wooden structure side by side, Buddy darted ahead. Boots paused to flip a light switch, though it didn't add much illumination to the space. Whickers greeted them, and a few horses stuck their heads over the stall doors to watch. She recognized her father's favorite horse, Red. A big sorrel with a white blaze, the horse neighed and stretched his neck.

"Your dad spoiled that dang pony."

Cass laughed and stepped over to the stall. Red nickered and stretched his nose toward her. She reached up, and his velvet lips nibbled her palm. "I'll sneak you a carrot later." She patted the horse's neck before glancing back at Boots. "So? You wanted me to see Red?"

He shook his head before tilting it toward the stall across the way. "Nope. I want you to look over here." He pointed to a stall across the barn. "Ben was a horse trader and that's what he did. Just for you."

Chance knocked on the door, but no one answered. Lights illuminated the windows and Boots's rusty old truck

was parked nearby. He walked to the end of the porch. A
glass of tea sweated on a metal table. Then he noticed the
open door and lights glowing in the barn. He sauntered
that way, rehearsing what to say. Whatever he said, his
heart wasn't really in what he had to do, even as it tripped
a couple of beats at the thought of seeing Cassidy again.

He stepped into the soft gloom of the barn and stopped
dead in his tracks.

Cassidy was leaning over a stable door murmuring
something he couldn't understand. The old man stood next
to her. Damn but she looked fine in jeans and boots. The
plaid flannel shirt tucked into those jeans enhanced every
one of her curves instead of hiding them. All the blood in
his head rushed south, and he had to lean on the barn door
to keep from pitching over face-first.

Boots opened the stall door, then they both disappeared
inside. Chance inhaled several times, adjusted the front of
his jeans and stepped deeper into the barn so he could see
what was in that stall.

"Good-lookin' colt you have there."

Cassidy jumped about a foot off the ground, whirled and
gasped, her face draining of color.

"You!"

He stepped back in mock innocence. "Me?"

"You! From Chicago!"

He held his hands, palms forward, out in front of him.
"Guilty. Though I have to admit Fate is being a lady today.
I figured I'd never see you again."

"What are you doing in Oklahoma?" Her brow furrowed,
and he decided her glare was one of the cutest expressions
he'd ever seen. Then again, there wasn't much about this
woman he didn't find attractive in one way or another.
That seemed to be the Barron family curse—they all had
a tendency to think with the wrong part of their anatomy

when a pretty woman was involved. He was far from immune from the affliction.

"I live here. What were you doing in Chicago?" As if they were playing poker, he called her furrowed brows with a sardonic grin and raised her with a wink.

"I live there." She sounded accusatory.

In all honesty, he rather enjoyed keeping her off balance. "So what brings you to Podunk, Oklahoma?" Cassie bristled, and color suffused her cheeks. He wondered if the same thing would happen if she were sexually aroused.

"Were you there this morning? At the memorial service?"

She'd seen him, dammit, just as he'd suspected. Well, he had no choice now. "Yeah. Why?"

"Pardon me for being a bit…suspicious. You try to pick me up in the hotel in Chicago then you follow me here and show up at my father's funeral. What's wrong with this picture?"

"Whoa, darlin'." She was a sarcastic little thing and damn if he didn't like it. A lot.

"Don't call me that. I don't even know your name."

"My name is Chance—Chancellor."

"Well, Mr. Chance Chancellor, you just turn around and walk right on out of here. I don't know who you are, why you're following me and frankly, I'm not sure I want to know. Get out and stay out!"

He blinked as his mind whirled. She'd cut him off before he finished his introduction. And now she was making assumptions about his name. Was it possible she didn't recognize him? That she had no clue he was a Barron? He wasn't sure if that bothered him. Okay, it did, but it simplified matters. He could figure things out before she ever guessed what was going on. "Easy, there, girl. I can explain."

"Oh? Really? And I'm not a girl, either."

No, she was definitely all woman. Her eyes positively

sparked energy, like two aquamarines under the noonday sun, and he shifted his stance to hide the effect she had on him. This was *not* the time to be thinking about getting her between the sheets. She was already suspicious of him, so he needed to walk very softly to gain her trust, and for some reason, that seemed very important to him.

No, he didn't need her trust; he needed her cooperation. He'd handled negotiations far more delicate in his career. He'd get Cassie into bed to get her out of his system then he'd move on, taking the deed to the ranch with him. That was the plan, and he needed to stick to it. Crossing the old man was not a smart thing to do, not when Cyrus Barron wanted something as bad as he wanted this place.

Then Chance inhaled. The dusty-sweet scent of Bermuda hay mixed with the musk-and-leather smell of horses. Rising above those, he caught a whiff of Cassidy—almond and cinnamon dancing with an underlying citrus tang.

"Yo, dude! Out of my barn. Now!"

Like a retriever coming out of a lake, he mentally shook to clear his mind. No distractions. Eye on the prize. But as she stood there, hands on her hips, forehead furrowed and chin jutting stubbornly, he realized she would always be a distraction. And that made him very nervous. No woman had ever gotten under his saddle like this one. His mouth curled into a slow smile, and he watched the effect on her— the slight dilation of her pupils, the flare of her nostrils and the swell of her chest. Yes, he could distract her, too. Good. The playing field was a bit more level now.

A not-so-polite hack and spit had them breaking their staring contest to glance at Boots. Chance recognized him now. Would the old man recognize him? Of all the Barron boys, he stayed out of the spotlight the most. Maybe he could slide through this as "Mr. Chancellor" after all.

"You here for a reason, son?"

Cass watched the stranger glance toward the stall, and

she could almost see the wheels turning in his head. Yes, he was sexy as all get-out, but she didn't trust him as far as she could throw that hunky six-foot-plus frame.

"Yessir. I came to see Ben's colt."

"I don't think we've met. How'd you know Ben?"

She cut her eyes to Boots. He didn't sound too put out, but she knew him. He was suspicious.

"I helped him locate the little guy. I own his half-brother. Same sire but from one of my mares. I considered buying this colt but didn't want to breed that close to the same bloodline."

She shifted her gaze from one to the other as they seemed to play a game of verbal ping-pong. She trusted Boots's instincts and for now she'd just let him run with the conversation. In the meantime, she could study Mr. Chance Chancellor. Tall, broad-shouldered and with a propensity for starched jeans and shirts, he looked like a model. But his boots were comfortably worn, if highly polished, and he wore that black Stetson on his head as if he'd been born to it.

If he traveled the rodeo or horse-show circuit, she'd lay odds he left a string of broken hearts in his wake. The hat covered his hair, but she remembered it being shiny, black and long enough to curl across his collar like the fingers of a lover. And his eyes. Amber, almost feral when the light hit them just right. His face? Chiseled. She had no other description for him. His cheekbones bordered on too angular but didn't cross the line. Plain and simple, he was gorgeous.

A vague memory pecked at her like one of the speckled hens searching the straw on the barn floor for a bite to eat. He still seemed familiar, but she couldn't place him. She'd figure it out eventually. She jerked out of her reverie when the guy took her hand and gave it a squeeze.

"I'm sorry for your loss, Miss Morgan."

"Cass. Everyone calls me Cass."

Her nose flared as if she couldn't inhale enough of his

warm scent. Leather and rain—a fragrance both homey and… Her insides tightened, but she refused to acknowledge the tiny quiver in the pit of her stomach. Well, a bit lower than that if she'd be honest with herself. This guy was sex on a stick, there was no denying it. But why was she being nice to him?

"On second thought, until you can prove you were a friend of my dad's, you can just call me Miss Morgan."

He laughed. Audacious and arrogant of him, but the sound reverberated in the barn and even Buddy came over to investigate. He sniffed at the man's boots, growled a little and hiked his leg.

"Buddy, no! Bad dog!" Her face flamed. Mortified that the dog was about to mark the man, she stammered an apology until Boots cut through her embarrassment.

"That dog has always had a good sense of people." He stared at Chance unblinking and for a moment, Cass wondered if Boots knew something she didn't. Her gaze darted between the two men, and tension in the barn ramped up a few degrees.

Buddy sat at her feet but his hackles rose, and she could feel the low growl rumbling in his chest as he leaned against her leg. Her father's old dog definitely did not like this man and apparently, neither did Boots. So why were her girlie bits going all fangirl on the guy?

"I think it's time for you to leave, Mr. Chancellor."

He dipped his chin and made a move to touch the brim of his Stetson. The gesture seemed old-fashioned and almost endearing. *Whoa, girl. Rein in that thought!*

"Another day then, Miss Morgan, when you aren't so stressed out or busy. Again, my condolences." He walked away but paused at the barn door. "We will see each other again, Cassidy Morgan."

Oh, hell. That dang sure sounded like a promise, but she wasn't sure just what the man had in mind.

Five

The office door clicked shut behind his secretary, but Chance had already swiveled in his chair to stare out the window. Restless energy roiled in his chest, leaving him unsettled. He wanted to see Cassidy again. And not because he wanted to serve her with legal papers. He wanted to spend time with her. Take her out and show her off.

What was it about this girl that riled him up? She invaded his thoughts, danced in his dreams and generally kept him guessing. He should stay away from her. She was bad news, and the old man would be royally pissed if he caught the barest whiff that Chance held any interest in Cass beyond his father's desire to crush her.

Screw it. He wanted to hear her voice. He could always say he was scoping out the competition if anyone in the family caught him. No one had to know what he was really thinking. Or feeling.

Chance scrolled through his contact list to the letter M. Not for the first time in the past few days, his finger hovered over the entry for Cassidy Morgan. He wanted to hit that call button so bad but he always stopped himself at the last instant—and not because he worried what the family would say.

What mattered was what Cass would say. How could he explain knowing her cell phone number? He'd called the ranch's landline once, only to hang up before anyone answered.

He finally gave up, shoved the phone in his jacket pocket and headed for the parking garage. He'd just drive out and see her.

Besides, he needed to check up on the colt, since he'd soon be a Barron asset. That was a good excuse. He'd also told Cass he would see her again, and to be honest, he'd enjoyed her quick intake of breath and the flash of her eyes when he made that promise. A grin twisted one side of his mouth. What Barron didn't keep his promises, right? Exactly. His driving out to see her this morning was now a matter of family honor.

Cassidy sat forward on the chair and watched the pickup rattle across the cattle guard and head up the dirt drive. She was alone, but for Buddy. The dog stayed behind when Boots had left first thing to run errands. Surprised when Buddy didn't jump up in the truck, Boots had shrugged and headed off. Cassidy had spent the morning mucking out stalls and making phone calls.

The loan officer at the bank seemed to be dodging her calls and try as she might, she'd been unable to hire a cattle hauler to get the herd to the stockyards in Oklahoma City. Every company she called told her to call back when the calves were ready to haul. What did she know about selling cows anyway? The cattle would be ready in May or early June. April was just rolling around.

And now Mr. Chancellor was pulling up in her front yard. Buddy leaped off the porch and charged the truck, dancing and barking as the driver's-side door opened and six-foot plus of sexy man stepped out. Since she'd last seen him, she'd done her best to convince her libido that the man was not nearly as hot as she remembered.

Her libido doubled over in laughter.

"What're you doin' here?" She had to yell over Buddy's excited barks.

Her visitor waded around the dog's determined forays to keep him away from the house and smiled. "A man can't come see a lady just because?"

"I'm not a lady, and I don't believe for a New York minute that you ever do anything *just because.*"

He pressed his hand against his chest. "You wound me, m'lady."

She rolled her eyes. "You are so full of it, dude, I'm glad I have my boots on." He laughed, and the sound did funny things to her insides.

"You going to make me stand out here in the sun, or can I come up and sit down?" The grin on his face challenged her as much as if he'd actually thrown down a gauntlet.

"Buddy, come." The dog responded to her instantly, but he never took his eyes off Chance. She returned to the little vignette of chairs and settled in her father's. She'd overcome her aversion and now sat there in the evenings, watching the sun go down and visiting with Boots. The dog hopped up into Boots's chair, and she chuckled. Sometimes, the Australian shepherd seemed almost human. She petted the dog and ignored the man as he clomped onto the porch and sat in the metal chair.

"Buddy looks like a little ol' cowboy sittin' there."

She glanced at the dog and laughed. His shoulders, chest and front legs were white. A black stripe circled his back and tummy and below that, his fur was speckled gray with black spots. His lower legs were tan, like he wore boots. A brown-and speckled-gray mask covered his eyes and ears.

"That or a bandit." She leaned back in her chair and stared at her guest. "So why are you here again, Mr. Chancellor?"

"Most people just call me Chance, since that's my name." The grin he flashed was devilish, and she wondered what thoughts were in his mind. "Fine. So, why are you here…Chance?"

"Can I be honest with you?"

"I don't know. *Can* you be honest?"

Damn but that question hit a little too close to home. Good thing he was the poker player in the family. Okay, honestly, he wouldn't want to play poker with any of his brothers. He deflected her question with a wink and a little smirk. "I'll plead the fifth on that one. You know what folks say, all's fair in love and war."

"Yeah, but which is this?"

"You tell me, Cassidy."

"You still haven't answered my question."

"Which one?"

"Well, you're a man so we know you can't be honest, so that leaves the other one. Why are you here?"

"Ow. I lodge a protest in the name of men everywhere." He offered her another crooked grin and a wink as he added, "I came to see you."

"Why?"

Time to lay his cards on the table. "Because I want to take you to dinner."

"Dinner."

"Yes, dinner. I know Boots goes to the Four Corners to eat. A lot. I figure you weren't kidding about being a bad cook. I'd like to take you out to eat. To a real restaurant." She folded her arms across her chest, and his eyes drifted despite his best efforts.

"Yo, dude. Eyes up here?"

Heat climbed the back of his neck. Was he actually blushing? He broadened his grin. "Sorry. A man can't help it when the view is so lovely." She snorted, and he laughed. He tossed a shrug of his shoulders into the mix and tried a boyish look on her. "The point remains. I'd still like to take you out."

"Like…on a date? A real date?"

"There's such a thing as a fake date?" She rolled her eyes again, and he couldn't tell if that was progress or not. "Yes, a real date. Dressing up and everything. A nice restaurant, maybe a movie after? Or we could go to Bricktown, hit some of the clubs?" Or maybe not. He'd be recognized there. Crap. He'd be recognized at any of his usual haunts. He needed a Plan B in a hurry. "Or we could go to my place, order in pizza and watch the Cubs game."

"Cubs? Are you kiddin' me?"

"Okay…White Sox?"

She looked disgusted. "Why do you think I'd be a fan of either one?"

"Um…you live in Chicago?"

"Yeah. But lifelong Cardinals fan here."

"Really? You *like* baseball?"

"Really. And I like *Cardinals* baseball."

"So, does that mean pizza at my place and the Cards on the big screen?" He liked that idea. His media room was that much closer to his bedroom, and he had every intention of seducing her before the date was over.

She snorted again. "How cheap do you think I am?" She eyed him speculatively. "Why should I go out with you?"

"I was attracted to you when we bumped into each other in Chicago. That hasn't changed."

Her lips pursed as she considered his offer; he wanted to kiss her but he'd remain patient. The time would come—sooner or later.

"Dinner at a nice place then a sports bar to watch the Cards."

She looked so cocky he couldn't help but grin back. For a brief moment, he toyed with the idea of calling up the corporate jet and flying her to St. Louis for the game. As a minority owner, Barron Entertainment had box seats, though he seldom got the chance to park his butt in them. Doing so would blow his cover, so he nodded in agreement. "Dinner out then a sports bar to watch the game. I'll pick you up around five? Game starts at 7:30." He stood up, and she looked startled.

"You're leaving?"

"Yeah, I got what I came for." Her expression changed, and he would have missed the flicker of sadness if he hadn't been studying her reactions.

"Well, don't let me keep you." She didn't move to stand. Instead, her hand gripped the arm of the chair as if to keep her in it. She wore an expression of studied casualness.

"Can you make coffee?" he suddenly asked. She stared at him like he was crazy. "We've established you can't cook. Does that mean you're a Starbucks baby, or can you perk a real pot of coffee?"

"I make excellent coffee, thank you very much. Even Uncle Boots doesn't complain."

Uncle Boots? This was a story he wanted to hear. "Then go make a pot, woman. Prove it to me."

"Ha! I made one just before you got here. So there." She darted up and through the door before he could react.

A few minutes later, she returned with a tray loaded with a clean mug, sugar bowl, creamer and a thermal carafe. "I figure you take your coffee black, but I admit to a sweet tooth and a need for cream."

Coffee steamed in his mug, and he inhaled the rich aroma. After a hesitant sip, he nodded. "This is good, but how do I know you made it?" She flushed, her anger rising quickly. He loved eliciting that reaction from her and couldn't wait to see what she was like when he had her in his arms.

"You'll just have to take my word for it."

Sparring with her was fun. He couldn't deny it. Most

women were dazzled by his last name. Cass had no clue, luckily. If she ever found out that his father wanted to take the ranch, she'd hate him. She could hate him later—after he'd given her a tumble, after he got her out of his system.

He finished off the coffee in his mug and reached for the carafe. His hand collided with hers, and instinct had him wrapping his fingers around hers. "Nice," he murmured.

"Mmm," she agreed.

As they chatted the afternoon away, clouds gathered on the western horizon. The rising temperature played with the white, puffy cumulous clouds until thunderheads billowed and thrust angry fists into the humid spring sky. A few formed the classic anvil shape associated with violent storms. Whatever breeze there'd been died, and the humidity thickened to the point it was almost hard to breathe.

"I don't remember a chance of t-storms mentioned on the weather last night." Cass stood and walked to the end of the porch, scanning the sky. "I'll be right back. You can come in if you want." She slipped into the house, and he followed.

Not sure what he had expected, Chance decided this wasn't it. The furniture might have been new when Cass was a child. Now it looked comfortably shabby. A clunky TV perched on a wooden bookcase and occupied the center of one wall. A metal stand with a saddle that seemed to be in the middle of repairs sat next to it. A leather couch and two ancient recliners formed a semicircle around a battered wooden coffee table made from a slab of pine and two small wooden wheels.

Cass pushed the power button on the TV and waited for the picture to form. Sure enough, one of the local weathermen spouted warnings as he stood in front of a radar image.

"Looks ugly."

She nodded. "Yeah, and headed this way." She walked closer and tapped the TV screen with her index finger. "See that? Hail core. I need to get the horses into the barn."

"I'll help."

"No, that's okay. Buddy and I can do it."

"Cass, I know horses. I can help."

She tossed a one-shouldered shrug in his direction, ducked around him and banged the screen door as she left. He glanced down at the dog. She'd banged the door in his face, too. "Wonder what we did wrong, boy?" The dog woofed, and the desultory wag of his tail might translate to a shrug, too.

"Well? You two coming or what?" Cassie's voice carried through the still air, punctuated almost instantly by a clap of thunder.

"Time to get a move on, Buddy. C'mon, boy." He opened the door and held it as the dog zipped out and launched off the porch, a gray blur headed straight for Cass. Chance followed at a trot. By the time he caught up, lightning flickered in the sky, and thunder rolled. The horses milled around a field on the other side of the barn.

"Get the barn door," Cassie yelled, but the rising wind tore her words away. She pointed, and he waved. She climbed the fence as Buddy ducked underneath the bottom rail.

Chance jogged to the barn, ducked inside and shut the door before heading to the far end. He noted the stall doors were already open and padded with fresh straw. He lifted the iron bar on the back door and pushed it open on well-greased rollers. He cut his gaze between the growing storm and the woman and dog working the horses up toward the barn. It was poetry in motion.

In the near distance, a sheet of rain filled the space between cloud and ground, marching across dusty fields. The first fat drops splattered in the dirt at his feet. He stepped out, prepared to help, then realized he might cause more problems by spooking the horses. While he wanted Cass to hurry, he knew she couldn't. She and Buddy were working the small herd like masters, but the storm galloped toward them.

The rain hit hard, and she was drenched immediately. The horses saw the open door and dashed inside. Chance had just enough time to step into the shadows as they charged in, Buddy hard on their heels. He rolled the door partially closed, leaving enough space for Cass to slip through. She darted in, looking as if she'd just climbed out of a pool. Her hair lay plastered to her head, and her white T-shirt, with the fitting slogan of "Take This Job and Shove It," did little to conceal every lacy stitch of her Victoria's Secret bra. He found that intriguingly incongruous. Despite her claims otherwise, Cassie Morgan was a cowgirl—but a cowgirl in a frilly Angel bra.

Chance closed the door, and the gloom in the barn deepened. His eyes adjusted, and he noticed the horses sorting themselves out and heading into stalls, with a little help from Buddy. Cass walked up one side shutting stall gates behind them. Chance took the other side and did the same. They met at the far end, and Cass flipped the light switch. He really wished she hadn't. He couldn't take his eyes from her curves. He began to unbutton his shirt.

"Whoa. Wait a minute there, cowboy. Just what the heck do you think you're doing?"

"You're wet."

"Um…duh."

"I'm dry."

"So?"

"So, either you're really happy to see me or you're cold." She glanced down, and when her gaze met his again, her cheeks were flushed. Oh, yes. She'd be delightful in bed. "I'm offering you my shirt."

She glowered at him. "You hardly seem the type to offer a girl the shirt off your back."

He peeled it off and handed it to her, amused that her

eyes widened, and her lips parted slightly. He got the distinct impression she liked what she saw when she licked her bottom lip. Of course the gesture created an interesting reaction behind the buttons of his jeans.

"Here." He waved the shirt a little, but she didn't seem to notice. His smile broadened, and he leaned closer to drape it over her shoulders. "There you go."

"Thanks…"

His lips hovered inches from hers and if she breathed deeply, her very perky nipples would brush against his bare chest. His fingers tangled in her hair as he smoothed the wet strands back from her face. Her eyes dilated, and she inhaled. Her chest swelled, and that's all it took. His lips found hers. He held her head still as his teeth nipped at her mouth. His tongue teased the seam of her lips until they parted for him. She tasted like café au lait, and he had an insane desire to fly her to New Orleans for beignets. Right after he kissed her senseless and made love to her for the rest of the afternoon.

She pressed against him, and he felt her shiver. He dropped one hand so he could encircle her waist with his arm and hold her closer. Like a contented cat, she rubbed and purred, her mouth open now and accepting the forays his tongue made against hers. While he kept his eyes open so he could watch her, she closed hers, as if lost in the moment. He liked that; liked the idea of sweeping her away, overriding her senses and making her his.

Cass was every bit as sexy as he remembered from their encounter in Chicago. He'd wanted to invite her up to his room and would have if not for that damn call from Cord. Just as he'd wanted to do then, his hand dropped to her round ass and he discovered it fit, filling his palm and making him horny as hell.

"I want you."

"Oh? Really?" She bumped against his erection and chuckled. "I hadn't noticed."

He ground his teeth together. "I didn't figure you for a tease, Cass."

She planted her hands against his chest and pushed a little. He dropped his arms. "I don't tease, Chance, not about sex."

"What about love?" She tilted her head and stared at him, unblinking. Where the hell had that come from? He didn't know, but he sure was curious about her answer.

"There's no such thing."

"Ooh. Cynical little thing, aren't you?"

"Yup, I am. What about you, Chance? I bet women tuck their phone numbers into those tight jeans of yours all the time. You're all about the sex, and I just don't see anything even remotely resembling love in that equation."

She backed up a step, putting some distance between them, but not so far he couldn't touch her if he wanted. Instead, he hooked his thumbs in the front pockets of his jeans and waited. The flash in her eyes convinced him she was just getting started, and he was curious about how far she would push.

"You tried to pick me up in the hotel in Chicago. You *knew* you'd never see me again. A one-night stand, that's all you were after. That's all you wanted."

She jabbed her finger in his chest, and the nail pricked a little, but then her fingertip caressed the spot before trailing down a couple of inches. Cass jerked her hand back as if she'd been burned and jutted her chin. He worked very hard to keep a poker face because inside, he was grinning madly.

"I bet you've never had a girl say no to you."

Well, no. I'm a Barron. They want to sleep with me for the name if nothing else. That thought hit a little too close to home, though he couldn't figure out why it bothered him.

"I bet *nobody* says no to you, in fact. You just…you have

that arrogant air of being all charmed and stuff. Like everything you touch turns to gold."

Pretty much. I'm a Barron, baby. It's genetic.

"Guys like you are a dime a dozen. Good-looking enough to be a male model, and you just skate by."

Not quite a dozen, darlin', unless the old man is hiding a few in the woodpile we don't know about.

"So why are you *here*? Why do you keep coming around?"

"Does this mean you aren't going out with me tonight?" He watched the flush creep up her neck, and he stepped toward her. Yes, he was a predator on the prowl, and she was his prey, but when she didn't back up, he had to give her points.

"What's that got to do with this discussion?"

"Discussion? Sounded more like a lecture to me, Cassidy. Why am I here? I came by to ask you out to dinner because I don't have your phone number. Why do I keep coming back? Because you're a damned attractive woman, and I want to get to know you. Is that so hard to believe?" He ignored the lie about her phone number, but all the other answers bounced around in his thoughts. And then the main one sucker punched him in the gut. *Because my father wants to ruin you, and I'm having trouble with that.*

She lowered her chin, and he didn't know if that was a good sign or a bad one. She blinked once. Twice. And a third time before her eyes narrowed. "Don't expect me to go all Sally Field at the Oscars here. I left my ego at the front gate. I don't trust you, Mr. Just-call-me-Chance. Not as far as I can throw you."

Cass paused to lick her lips, and that's all it took. He wrapped his hands around her biceps and pulled her to him. He kissed her, taking her mouth by storm. She resisted for a long moment then relented, her tongue teasing his lips this time. He could feel her heartbeat, and was thrilled it galloped as fast as his own. His pulse pounded in his ears, every bit as loud as the thunder outside the barn.

Her arms slipped around his neck, and he backed her up to the nearest wall without breaking the kiss. Heat flared between them, and he brushed his shirt off her shoulders. He could feel the rasp of the lace on her bra through her T-shirt.

"Too many clothes." He growled the words as he peeled the wet cotton over her head and then sealed his lips against hers again. One hand roamed down to stroke her thigh and just as he hoped, she rubbed her knee up his leg. He cupped her sweet ass and the next thing he knew, she'd wrapped those long legs around his waist. He couldn't breathe for a minute as the most intimate part of her cradled his erection.

Chance broke the kiss to gasp for breath and leaned his forehead against hers. "Baby, you are so hot but dammit, I want to make love to you in a bed."

She froze. "What?"

Well, hell. He was definitely thinking with the wrong head at the moment. "Yeah. Our first time. I want it to be right. I'd take you standing here just like this, but I want to take it slow. I want to watch you come apart in my arms before I sink in. I want to touch you and kiss you and find out just how many times I can make you come before you beg me to stop."

Six

What the heck was she doing? Cass couldn't think straight and wasn't sure she wanted to. Her wet bra chafed her sensitized nipples but instead of irritating, the sensation sent waves directly to the area of her body presently rubbing against Chance's fly. He was as turned on as she was; a definite plus, and the things he was saying left her panting. Some part of her consciousness didn't trust him, but her libido didn't care. He was sexy and hot for her. His body promised things to hers, and waiting was killing her. She'd never been known for her patience.

"Shut up and kiss me."

"Yes, ma'am."

"Talkin—mmmmmm."

His mouth took her breath away and cut off any more talking on her part, too. Chance pressed closer, his erection rubbing against her as he pushed her a little higher on the wall to change the angle. If they'd been naked, she'd be riding him hard and fast. Her tongue pushed his aside and thrust into his mouth. He gripped her head with gentle hands and dragged his mouth from hers only to trail his tongue down her neck and across her collarbone.

Cass sighed and arched her head back. She rested it against the wood behind her, leaving her neck exposed to his attentions. With a little space between them now, one of his hands cupped her. She inhaled sharply, which pushed her breast deeper into his palm. He groaned, and she tightened her legs around his waist, all but sealing them together.

"Want to taste you." His words burst out in puffs of his breath. "Want to touch you."

"Talking. You're talking again."

"I think there should be a whole lot more talkin' goin' on and a whole lot less touchin'."

Mortified, she gasped and stared over Chance's shoulder. Boots stood in the barn doorway, hands on his hips, his face perfectly blank. Chance hunched against her, and she tapped him on the shoulder. "Yo, dude...company?" She cut her eyes to indicate they'd been caught.

Chance glanced over his shoulder and flashed a wicked grin. "He doesn't have a shotgun, so I think we're safe."

She thumped him on the shoulder. "Put me down, Chance."

"You're the one with your legs wrapped around my waist, darlin'."

She felt heat rise up her chest and flood her face. With her hands on his shoulders for leverage, she unhooked her ankles and dropped first one foot then the other to the floor. Her knees threatened to buckle but with a gallant gesture, Chance supported her until she got her bearings. Dizzy, out of breath and blushing furiously, she managed to face Boots from behind Chance's brawny frame.

"Busted, Uncle Boots. I...sort of figured you wouldn't be back until after the storm."

"Storm's been over awhile, Cassidy." His expression didn't change—remaining stony with a spark of anger lighting his eyes.

"I got a little wet getting the horses in. Chance offered me his shirt." Of course, his shirt was on the floor, along with hers. That elicited a quirked brow from the older man. She sucked in a deep breath and reached for her inner adult.

"If you don't mind, Uncle Boots, we'll see you up at the house in a few minutes."

Boots glanced at his watch, stared at her then favored Chance with a scowl. "Five minutes or I'm coming back. With Winnie."

As the old man exited the barn, Chance cut his eyes to her. "Winnie?" His whisper raised goose bumps on her rapidly chilling flesh.

"Winnie is his Winchester shotgun."

"We'll be right behind you, sir."

A giggle burbled up from nowhere at Chance's quick reply, and she hissed out, "It's not like he'll make you marry me or anything."

The man in front of her stilled. Completely, totally, not-even-breathing stilled. As quick as a snake, his head whipped around, and his eyes bored into hers. She choked off another giggle and stared back, wide-eyed and startled.

"That's a joke, Chance." She reached for him but seeing his expression, her hands plummeted to her sides like rocks.

"Marrying me would be a joke?"

Cass pressed back against the wall. This was a side of him she'd never guess at, and one that scared her just a little. This was a man used to getting everything he wanted. "No." Her brain whirled as she searched for the words to get her out of this. Where had this intensity come from? Why did he look both angry and hurt? They hadn't even gone on a date yet—making out in the barn did not count.

"Shotgun wedding, Chance. That's the joke. Us getting married? You have to admit that's a bit far-fetched. We just met. And besides, just because I took a leave of absence from my job doesn't mean that I'm not going back to Chicago once I get the ranch squared away."

He trapped her with his hands braced against the wall on either side of her head. "What's that mean?"

"What do you think it means? I live in Chicago, Chance.

I have a good job there. Friends. A life that's not here on a ranch. I plan to sell Dad's cattle, settle his debts and sell this place if I can so I can take care of Boots. And Buddy. Maybe a couple of the horses. Find a couple of acres where they'll be happy." She lifted one shoulder in a negligent shrug. "I'm not a cowgirl."

"So…going out with me is basically a one-night stand for *you*?"

She furrowed her brow as he tossed her own words back in her face. His attitude totally confused her. "You're getting way ahead of yourself, Chance. Yeah, we generate some heat, but it's just sex." She stared at him, trying to read his expression. "Isn't it? We don't know each other well enough for it to be anything else."

He pressed closer, crowding her, and she almost got dizzy from lack of oxygen. Cass inhaled sharply, ducked under his arm and slipped into the tack room. She emerged wearing a windbreaker and bent over to snag her T-shirt and his work shirt, which she tossed in his direction. "I'll be ready at five if you still want to take me out. If you don't show up, I'll understand."

With as much dignity as she could muster, she pivoted and marched to the door. Luckily, Boots had left it open, and she managed to step outside without tripping. The storm was gone, the black, roiling clouds with jagged lightning pushing on to the east, leaving wet grass and mud behind. Buddy dashed past her and raced to the house, leaving her to follow a bit more sedately in his path despite the fact she wanted to run.

When she arrived at the house, her boots clumped on the wooden steps and across the porch. The porch door banged behind her. She could hear Boots rummaging in the kitchen. She headed straight to her room. A hot shower and dry clothes would give her perspective on things. She hoped. Because at the moment, she was completely clueless as to what had just happened.

Chance watched Cassie walk away. What the hell had come over him? He was not the possessive type, and a one-night stand was his hookup of choice. No ties, no needy females. So how had he gone from cocky cowboy to the one clinging and needing reassurance of the relationship? As Cass said, what relationship? Dammit all to hell. He needed to get her into his bed so he could get her out of his system. Plain and simple.

Only it wasn't. Neither plain, nor simple. The time had come for him to think about work, not the sexy woman driving him crazy. Besides, what did it matter? Cassie was going back to Chicago. She didn't want to stay here. She didn't want to be with him.

He rubbed the spot over his chest as he climbed into his truck. He didn't start it right away, but instead sat and stared at the window he figured was Cassie's bedroom. The place wasn't big. Hell, his condo had more square footage than the farm house. The furniture was old, dilapidated, lived in. Loved.

And there was his answer. That house was filled with love. A kind of love he and his brothers had missed out on growing up. Cassie was three when she lost her mother, but her daddy had loved her. And her Uncle Boots. For the first time in his life, Chance was jealous. It was an emotion that would take some getting used to.

He started the truck, backed up until he had room to turn around and headed toward the main road. He had a lot to think about.

Cassie waited until she heard Chance drive away before she kicked off her boots and peeled out of her wet jeans. The man was a player. She knew that with every feminine

instinct she possessed. Serial daters. That's what her best
friend in Chicago called guys like him. Hopping from bed
to bed. Their smart phone containing a contact folder simply labeled "Easy." The last thing she needed or wanted
was to hook up with an Oklahoma cowboy, even if he had
a fine ass, gorgeous build and a face that could melt the
South Pole. Cowboys wanted cowgirls, and she no longer
fit that description.

Standing in her bra and panties damp from more than
rain, she turned a slow circle. Her room. Which hadn't
changed a bit since she left for college ten years before.
Trophies and buckles littered the top of her dresser with
a couple of framed photographs stuffed among them. In
one, she stood next to Barney, her first horse. She barely
reached the top of his front leg, despite the hat jammed on
her head. She proudly held her first championship buckle,
even though she hadn't even been big enough to mount Barney without a boost at the time. In another, she sat behind
her dad's saddle, her arms around his waist. In a third, she
posed with a saddle she'd won.

A tap on her door sent her scrambling for her robe. She
shoved her arms through the worn flannel sleeves and tied
it at her waist. "C'mon in, Uncle Boots."

The door swung open, creaking a little. "We need to
talk, baby girl."

Cass nodded. "Let me grab a shower first?"

He nodded, turned and shuffled down the hall to the living room. She dashed to the bathroom. Though she would
have preferred to stand there until the hot water tank emptied, she showered quickly and dressed in clean jeans and
a fresh T-shirt. When she was ready, she went out to the
living room and settled on the couch. Boots sat in his recliner looking uncomfortable. Cass wet her bottom lip with
a nervous swipe of her tongue and felt way too much like
a teenager caught making out.

"You still planning on selling out?"

Selling *out*? That sounded almost ugly, and disloyal—and not at all what she anticipated for a topic. "I'm not a rancher, Uncle Boots. I need to sell the place to pay Daddy's debts. And to give you a cushion so you can find a little place."

"This ain't about me, Cassidy. This is about you. About the heritage your daddy left for you. About who you are deep down."

She clasped her hands together and shoved them between her knees as she leaned forward. Staring at her bare toes, she gathered her thoughts. "I'm not a cowgirl, Uncle Boots. Haven't been since I left for college."

"Then why did you go round up the horses when the storm hit?"

"Because it needed doing."

"Would a city girl have gotten soakin' wet to move them into the barn?"

"Just because I knew what was the right thing to do doesn't mean I want to run this ranch."

Boots leaned back and stared out the front window. "Ben went lookin' for a colt. A very special colt. For you." He held up his hand when she started to speak, and his words cut through any argument she might offer. "Just hush up and listen, Cassidy." His eyes returned to the scenery outside. The silence stretching between them wasn't comfortable, but Cass remained quiet.

"Your daddy knew you didn't want to stay here. He hoped you would, but he knew deep down that you had to go off and see the world. He did the same thing." He glanced in her direction. "He lived on the road for a good many years. And then he met your momma. She put down roots here. Deep ones. Then you came along. So he settled down. He built this place fence post by fence post. At one time, Morgan-Baxter Rodeo Company supplied stock for all the big rodeos. Calgary. National Finals. Las Vegas. Denver. We even made it to Madison Square Garden one year. Your daddy was a name, honey. But he didn't want you to be a cowgirl."

Her mouth gaped open. "Well, you damn sure could have fooled me!"

Boots chuckled softly. "He wanted more for you. He wanted you to be a rancher. Or a trainer. Or a breeder. Even as a kid, you had an uncanny sense about horses, baby girl. But at the same time, he knew you had the same wander-lust in your blood he did. So he waited for you to get it out of your system. And then he found that colt. Legend's Double Rainbow."

Memory flared—her dad driving Cass in his truck as he explained her mom wasn't coming home and a double rainbow arching across the sky in front of them. She stared at the old man, confused. "He bought this stud colt just because of his name?"

Boots laughed. At her. "Honey, you know your daddy better than that. That little fella has a pedigree going all the way back to Leo." A sly look crossed his face.

She blinked, her mind skipping everything but the name *Leo*. "Wait…Leo? As in the foundation stallion?"

He nodded. "Yep. He found a colt with a bloodline that traces straight back to Leo."

"Holy cow!" Leo was a legendary quarter horse stud. He had produced racehorses, the finest performance horses and more than a few rodeo champs along the way. She leaned back, possibilities whirling through her mind despite her intentions. No. She had to think about Chicago. Her life was in Chicago. Not here on some dirt-road ranch. Wasn't it?

Her brow furrowed in consternation as another thought intruded. She leaned forward. "How the hell did he pay for the colt? I…I can't even imagine how much he's worth!"

"Your daddy was a born horse trader, baby girl."

She processed that statement, her chest tight with dread. She didn't want to, but she asked, "What did he do?"

"Your daddy had one of the finest collections of rodeo memorabilia anywhere outside of the Western Heritage Museum. Turns out Doc's former owner is a collector."

"Wait. Doc?"

Boots nodded. "The colt. They call him Doc for short."

She had to think about that a minute before the initials DR—for Double Rainbow—occurred to her. "Oh! Sorry. I'm slow. I'm still…Daddy had a collection?"

He laughed. "Neither of us would have called it that, but the attic and the loft in the barn were filled to the rafters with stuff. Your daddy was a pack rat. He never threw anything away. This ol' boy drove all the way down from Illinois towin' a big ol' trailer with the colt inside. He sorted all the boxes, loaded up his trailer and left Doc in trade. Ben figured it was a good deal." His eyes misted. "I think he knew he was dyin' but wasn't ready to surrender to the damn cancer. Ben probably figured neither of us would want to sort all that stuff."

Boots stared out the window. He didn't look at her as he continued. "Your daddy wanted to leave you something, baby girl. A legacy. A way to find your own roots, and he hoped you'd put those roots down here."

Cass sucked in a long breath and held it a moment to ease the tightness in her chest. It didn't help. Despite the burning tears filling her eyes, she managed to choke out the words. "I didn't know how bad he was, Uncle Boots. I should have come sooner."

"He didn't want you to know, hon. He even hid it from me for a long time. But gettin' ahold that little stud was his final gift to you. It's up to you, Cassidy Anne. What are you going to do with it?" The old man's eyes twinkled as winked at her. "And what are you gonna do about that young buck sniffin' around you in the barn?"

Seven

Chance pulled up in the yard and parked. He sat for a moment, feeling far too much like a high school boy on his first date. The fact they'd been caught all but *in flagrante delicto* in the barn that afternoon didn't bother him. But the look Boots had given him did. The old man knew who he was, but Chance could not figure out why he hadn't told Cass. He needed to have a little chat with Boots Thomas.

His cell phone chimed, and he glanced at the caller ID. Barron Security—Cash calling from the office. He answered with a blunt, "What's up?"

"I've been following up on the paper trail on that colt the old man wants."

Chance rubbed his forehead. He'd all but forgotten about the colt between his efforts to dodge filing the lawsuit to foreclose on the ranch and reining in his wayward thoughts about the woman he was supposed to ruin. "This couldn't wait until morning?"

"You're sitting at Ben Morgan's place, aren't you?"

"Dammit, Cash. Are you tracking me?"

"What do you think? Gotta love built-in GPS on the smartphones."

Grimacing at the virtual leash, Chance steered the conversation back the subject. "What about the colt?"

"Registration papers just popped up with the AQHA. Ownership's been transferred. To Cassidy Morgan. Makes me wonder how a horse the old man had in his sights suddenly pops up in her name, and that makes me curious about her interest in you, bro."

Chance considered the possibilities. He'd seen her face in the barn when Boots showed her the colt. She'd seemed surprised. If he ever had to play cards with someone, he wanted it to be Cass. She had the worst poker face in the world. Besides, how would she or her father know that Cyrus was after the same horse? The facts just didn't add up. Sure, women always had angles to get close to or take advantage of the Barron brothers. He didn't believe Cassie was one of them.

"Who signed off on the registration? American Quarter Horse Association doesn't require a principal to file the papers."

"Former owner, as her agent."

He pondered that information, still not convinced of her culpability. "Doesn't mean she knew it was happening."

"Why are you defending her, Chance? Wait, don't tell me. She's pretty, and you're a sucker for a damsel in distress."

"Shut up, Cash."

"Then why haven't you filed the paperwork dealing with calling in the loan and preserving the collateral?"

"Are you checking up on me?"

"Just following the old man's orders, big brother. Which is something you'd better start doing. He wants that land and the colt. Cassidy Morgan has both. You've been jackin' around too long and spending way more time sniffing around that little gal than in your office taking care of business. It's time to get in, kill two birds with one stone and get the hell out. Simple."

Simple? Chance closed his eyes and rubbed his forehead again. Nothing about Cassidy Morgan was simple. Nothing about this acquisition was simple. Once upon a time, life had been. He'd wanted to ride the rodeo circuit, then settle down to run the family cattle business and breed some excellent horses on the side. Unfortunately, the old man had different ideas. He'd steered each of his sons into a profession. A short bark of laughter escaped at the thought. Cyrus Barron didn't steer. He bullied, hammered, demanded and dragged his sons kicking and screaming all the way. His old man always got what he wanted.

Movement on the front porch caught his attention. Boots stepped to the rail, staring at him. "I gotta go, Cash."

"Just get it done, Chance."

Opening the door, he stepped out of the truck and met Boots halfway to the house. The older man squared off, hands on his hips, jaw jutting, looking a bit like a bulldog ready to defend his territory.

"I just have one thing to say to you, boy."

Chance bristled. No one, not even his father called him *boy*. "Then say it, old man."

"You hurt that little gal, I'll hunt you like the junkyard dog I know you are."

Chance rocked back, surprised by the direction this conversation had taken.

"I recognized you, Chance Barron, when you walked into the barn that first time. And I know all about the bad blood between her daddy and yours."

"Then why haven't you told Cass?"

"Because I haven't figured out your angle. Given what I saw this afternoon, maybe you do have feelings for her. That said, I don't have to like you, and I dang sure don't have to trust you." Boots glanced toward the house then looked him up and down. "You better tell her who you really are. She's just like her daddy—never could abide a liar."

"I'm not…" His voice trailed off. He wasn't a liar. He might not tell the whole truth, or he might bend it, but he didn't lie. Besides, he wasn't under oath. He lifted one shoulder in a negligent shrug. "Does it matter, Mr. Thomas? She's headed back to Chicago soon anyway."

"Maybe."

Chance stared, wondering about the cryptic reply. As an attorney, he was used to having all the aces up his sleeve. He'd been half a step behind since seeing Cass at that hotel in Chicago. "As far as I know, she intends to go back to her job. They won't give her compassionate leave forever."

The front door opened, and Cass stepped out. He stood transfixed, the conversation with Boots forgotten. Her blond hair looked like spun silk, and the light shining from the house bathed her in a halo. This was the first time he'd seen her wearing anything remotely feminine—besides those killer boots in Chicago. The skirt she wore hugged her hips and left her long legs in plain sight. A lacy turquoise tank left just enough of the rest of her to the imagination. He swallowed. Hard. Ignoring Boots, he stepped toward her.

"Wow." She smiled, and he gulped again. "You look terrific."

Her cheeks pinkened, and she dropped her gaze. When she looked up, her eyes twinkled and crinkled at the corners. "Happy to see you, too, cowboy."

He was so busted. She laughed at the expression on his face when he figured out what she meant. He *was* happy to see her. And she was happy to see him. She couldn't remember the last time a guy turned her on like Chance. Her breasts swelled as she inhaled. Just thinking about the kiss they'd shared had her all but panting. She cut her eyes to look at him and noticed his gaze dropped to her chest. She cleared her throat, and his head jerked up, his expression guilty as he met her eyes. She bit back a laugh. Busted again, but she didn't mind.

He made her feel sexy and desirable, so she made a bit

of a show when she fastened her seat belt. Oh, yeah. He noticed.

"So, where are you taking me to dinner?"

He had to lick his lips before he spoke. Yes, her outfit definitely had the desired effect. She'd been ready to make love to him in the barn. She was more than ready to explore that aspect of things as soon as they finished dinner.

He started the truck and maneuvered it back toward the road before he glanced over, gave her an appreciative smile and replied. "I thought we'd go to Old Chicago." She flashed a "you've got to be kidding me" face at him and he laughed. "You have to admit, it's fitting, all things considered."

Cass rolled her eyes but resisted sticking out her tongue. "Well, if that's the case, I should have dressed for comfort..." She liked teasing him.

"Actually, I thought we might head down to Bricktown. Since you haven't been home in a while, I think you'll be surprised."

"Any place in particular?"

He chuckled. "Well, Toby Keith's place makes great chicken-fried steak."

"And this is your idea of a big date?"

"You've never seen the size of that chicken fry."

She laughed. "Okay. We'll go eat at Toby's. I'm starved."

After dinner—which included chicken-fried steak the size of a plate—Chance suggested a walk along the Bricktown canal. Amazed, Cass stared at the renovated brick factory buildings, the lights, the bustle of the crowd. Boats cruised by, and she caught snatches of the drivers' patter as they pointed out the sights to those on the tour.

Chance held her hand as they strolled. Nerves had nothing to do with her excitement. This was all about the sparks of sexual tension first ignited in the barn. Yet if she was honest, there was something more. Something deeper. Heck yeah, this man turned her on, but at the same time she felt a connection to him. When she fantasized about being with him, it wasn't…sex. Oh, it was sexy. Sexy as hell, but it was more. She wanted more. She wanted to make love to him. She wanted to explore that tenuous bond developing between them.

Cass glanced up, realized he'd been watching her and had to resist the urge to fan her face. She really wished her face didn't betray her moods so easily. He squeezed her hand and tugged her closer to him. Stopping in the middle of the walk, they forced people to step around them. She didn't care.

She'd never been in love, didn't have a clue what it felt like. Lust? Oh, yeah. She knew all about that flash-in-the-pan heat that burned hot and fast between a man and a woman. And dissipated just as quickly. With this man, though, it was a slow burn like banked embers radiating heat. Cass raised her face, and he obliged her by dropping a gentle kiss on her lips.

They stared at each other, ignoring both snickers and rude remarks from the people they blocked. She wanted to get lost in his eyes, in his arms, despite the prickle of unease tapping on her shoulder. Her parents had loved deeply, and her dad's world had shattered when her mom died. Only three when it happened, she remembered the crushing sadness—even now. And she wondered. Was that why she'd never let go? Never fully trusted a man enough to let him into her heart?

Could *this* man be the one? She didn't know him. But she did. On some deep level, she recognized their connection. Not that she believed in soul mates or anything. But her parents' relationship had been soul-deep and abiding. And love at first sight, according to her mother's diaries.

Chance didn't move. He watched Cass, curious about

her thoughts. Emotions danced across her face, changing her expressions. Her soft gaze held him mesmerized. Time seemed to stop, and he was afraid to do anything that might break the mood. He wanted to capture the smile she offered him—hold it and save it in a wooden box where it would be safe. That smile was a treasure greater than anything in his family's bank vault.

A couple of college kids brushed past them and one of them muttered, "Get a room."

With the spell broken, Chance led Cassie back to the lot where he'd parked his truck, guided her inside and lingered a moment with the door open. He leaned in, and his lips brushed across hers.

"Now or never, darlin'. We goin' back to my place or am I takin' you home?"

"Your place." Not a moment's hesitation there. She wanted him—his hands on her bare skin, and hers on his. She wanted to explore him with her fingertips, learn his contours. She wanted to kiss him. All over. She remembered to breathe.

"My place." The words came out in a possessive growl.

The drive was a blur, but she vaguely noted it when he pulled the truck into some sort of garage. As he rushed her to an elevator, she caught a glimpse of a dark metallic sports car parked back in the shadows—one that looked expensive. The elevator doors slithered open, and he urged her inside. He was a condo cowboy, and that made her giggle. He arched a brow but didn't say anything, or kiss her. He'd snugged her close to his side right after he hit the floor button but made no other moves. She could feel his heartbeat against her arm, and his quickened breath ruffled her hair.

The doors parted, and they got out. Chance fumbled with the door lock but managed to finally get it open. He ushered her inside, kicked the door shut with a booted foot and grabbed her—not roughly, but with force. Again she was struck by the gentle strength in his big hands as they wrapped around her upper arms. He tugged her to him. Her breasts collided with the muscular wall of his chest as his lips sealed against hers. He kissed her hard, his mouth hungry and demanding, and he sucked her breath away before his lips gentled and he angled his head, nibbling her lips like they were dessert. He sighed—actually sighed— and kissed his way along her jaw. Her knees trembled, and his grip slipped from her biceps as his arms encircled her. Her arms snaked around his neck, and she tilted her head up for more kisses.

"Cards game?" His voice sounded a little breathless.

"What game?" So did hers.

Chance scooped her into his arms and carried her to the bedroom. She caught a glimpse of the city skyline out the window before he hit a button and the drapes slithered close. One small part of her brain, the part still semicoherent and sane, wondered at the high tech but he kissed her again, and all reason disappeared.

Undressing devolved into a frenzy of buttons, zippers and tossed clothes. Naked, panting for breath, they stared at each other, eyes roving appreciatively. Cass blushed and dropped her gaze for a moment. She wasn't a model by any stretch of the imagination. Curvy. A real woman, not a stick figure. That's what she was and despite Hollywood, she would embrace her body. She squared her shoulders and raised her head. The heat from Chance's gaze almost rocked her backward. He licked his lips while he clenched and unclenched the fists at his sides, as if he was struggling to hold them there to keep from touching her.

"You. Are. Even. More. Beautiful. Than I ever dreamed." Each word huffed out as he panted, with the last ones rushing out in a gasp.

Before she could react, he advanced. His arms slid around her, pulled her close so her nipples brushed against the fine feathering of hair on his chest. Her tummy bumped up against something long, thick and hard. She arched and rubbed against his erection, and he groaned against her neck, distracted from the kisses he'd been planting there.

"Keep that up, and I won't be able to. Keep up, I mean."

She chuckled. "I'm a firm believer in—" She couldn't get the last word out. He pushed her back against the bed until her knees buckled. He eased her down, his lips sealed on hers, and then dragged her across the linen bedspread. He didn't bother turning down the covers.

"You first." He positioned her legs, knees up, and spread them. He stared at her for a long moment, and she fought the urge to press them together. He stretched out, his head between her thighs. His gaze caught hers, held it, and then he growled again.

"Mine."

Cass arched off the bed as his tongue tasted her. She was already primed and ready and at this rate, she wouldn't last long. His fingers teased her as he lapped at her bud. Incoherent now, she could only utter muffled moans and little panting whimpers. Every muscle in her body quivered, and her hips danced beneath him until his long fingers gripped her thighs to hold her still. With the gusto of a connoisseur, he kissed and licked, his fingers tantalizing her.

He raised his head. "Come for me, baby. Show me what I do to you, Cass." He inserted another finger, and his touch taunted her.

"No…no…no…"

"Yes."

That one word was an order she eagerly complied with, her eyes squinting shut as emotions and sensations overwhelmed her. Pressure built in her middle and if she didn't pop that cork, she would shatter. In the end, that's what she did anyway. The power of her climax tossed her into a sparkling tunnel, and she rode through it for a full minute before she shattered.

Cass wanted to cry and laugh at the same time. She'd never had a climax that rocked her so deeply. Chance kissed her down there before trailing kisses up her tummy and between her breasts all the way to her lips. His arms cradled her, and he stroked down her back as his kiss gentled her raging emotions.

"I'd ask if it was good for you, but I already know."

She thumped his chest but it was a feeble blow. "Holy cowboy. That was…" She inhaled and her breath hitched a couple of times as little aftershocks zinged all the way to her fingers and toes.

He laughed—a deep, throaty sound like a happy growl. Her head found the niche of his shoulder and seemed to fit. She curled in at his side, her fingers ruffling the soft hair on his chest. There was just enough there to play with so she did. In comfortable silence, they held each other. She'd almost dozed off when she shifted her knee over his thigh. And encountered his arousal. She shivered, and goose bumps prickled her skin.

Cass skimmed her palm down his chest and across some amazing ridges that defined his abdomen. Forget six-pack abs. This guy was at least an eight if not a twelve. When her questing fingers encountered his erection, his hips arched, and he groaned.

"If you touch me now, I won't last."

Her face crinkled with glee. "Oh? I guess that means I have you at my mer—" She choked on the last word as Chance grabbed, flipped and settled his brawn on top of her.

"I want to be inside you. We'll play later."

"I don't ride bareback."

He reached into a drawer next to the bed and withdrew a shiny packet. "Neither do I. Do you want the honors?"

"Um…awkward. Nope. I leave it up to your expert hands."

He grinned, ripped the top of the packet with his teeth and…*oh, yeah*. He definitely had expert hands. Cass had never found this particular part of lovemaking sexy, but what he did with his hands left her panting and wanting more. He stroked himself as he stroked her, and she arched her hips.

"Anytime now, cowboy."

"Yes, ma'am."

That was the last coherent thought she had for a very long time. He sank in, and she gasped. He filled her comfortably and once in, he withdrew almost immediately. Her inner muscles clenched around him, and she wrapped her legs around his waist to keep him inside. She found the rhythm, matched and expanded it, and succumbed to the sensations surging along her neural paths. She hoped they didn't short-circuit her brain. Then she hoped they would. Then she just didn't care, totally lost in the sensation of Chance driving into her. The muscles on his back bunched under her hands, and she cinched her legs tighter, as if she were riding a bucking bronco. His breath whooshed out, and she swore she could feel him swell and grow larger. A switch triggered deep inside her, and she spiraled up and out of control.

They came together, and lights sparkled behind her closed eyelids. She shivered and felt an answering shudder from him as he pushed against her, riding slowly now as he milked the last bit of passion from them both. Sated, sleepy and more contented than she'd felt in…forever, she nuzzled his neck, smiling at the salty taste of his skin.

He kissed her temple and pushed against the restraint her legs formed around his waist. "I'm too heavy." The words came out mumbled.

She opened her eyes. He looked like she felt, and that

made her smile even bigger, but she unhooked her ankles. Her legs quivered and dropped like logs to the bed. He rolled to his side and pulled her close, one hand caressing her hip and thigh.

"I'd ask if it was good for you, but I'd have to form a coherent thought to talk."

He laughed and kissed her forehead. "Yeah."

"Spoken like a true caveman."

"Baby, if it got any better, I don't think I'd survive."

She propped up on her elbow and smirked. "You ain't seen nothin' yet, cowboy." She licked her lips in a show of bravado, relishing that his eyes tracked her tongue. She finished the gesture by tapping the tip of her tongue against her top lip, as if she licked something else entirely. His gratifying groan elicited a laugh. "Oh yeah, buddy. Just you wait. The night is young."

He smirked back. "Be careful what you ask for, darlin'. A challenge like that might just jump up and bite you on the ass."

Eight

Cass drowsed in Chance's arms, content but all too aware she needed to get up, get dressed and get him to drive her home. She had chores to do. Since coming home, she'd pitched in to ease the burden on Boots. He was older than her father, and while he looked hale and hearty, he was seventy. He didn't need to be wrestling bales of hay or mucking stalls. And truthfully, she really didn't want him to know she'd spent the night with Chance. Feeling way too much like a delinquent teen, she slipped out of the circle of arms holding her. Tiptoeing across the room, she shut the door to the bathroom before flipping on the light.

The reflection staring back at her from the mirror showed a woman who'd been well and truly loved. Swollen lips, a slightly abraded cheek—darn his shadow beard— half-lidded eyes and hair that looked like a windstorm had blown through. She ran cold water from the faucet and splashed her face. Using her finger as a toothbrush, she attempted to freshen her breath. But when it came to her hair, running her fingers through it only created more snags. Talk about a major case of bed head. Reluctant to rummage through his drawers or medicine cabinet, though denying her curiosity almost killed her, she flipped off the light and opened the door—only to run smack dab into a muscular chest.

"You're up early."

She tilted her head to look up at him. "Sorry. Didn't mean to wake you, but now that you are...I need to go home, 'kay?"

His eyes narrowed. "No, not okay. Why?"

"I have chores."

He blinked at her and rubbed a hand across his face as if clearing the last bit of sleep befuddlement from his head. "Chores?"

"Chores. At the ranch. Horses to feed. Cows to feed. Stalls to muck. You're a cowboy." She glanced around, curious now about the luxury condo. "Allegedly. Surely you've done ranch work before?"

He scratched his chest, an idle gesture that drew her gaze. She inhaled sharply, her nostrils flaring as his scent filled her. Musk, leather and something clean—like fresh laundry hanging on a clothesline on a hot summer day. She almost laughed at the thought. *No* one smelled like sunshine.

"Want to grab a shower? We can share, save time and water?"

"Do you really think the two of us in the shower will save time?"

"Well, we could do it with you sitting on the counter, but I sort of like wet and wild." He backed her into the bathroom and flicked on the light. "Won't be as thorough as I'd like, but it'll take the edge off."

He reached around her, turned on the shower and before she could protest, picked her up and stepped under the myriad jets. He set her down, grabbed a bottle of body wash and started in. By the time he finished, she was clean, sated and weak-kneed. Then again, so was he. Two could play that game.

She forked the last bit of new straw into Doc's stall and turned around. Chance stood there watching her. Tilting her head, she cocked her hand on a hip and gave him her best sassy smile. "See something you like, cowboy?"

"Mmm-hmm."

Cass had to admit he'd surprised her. He didn't drop her off. He'd parked his truck and insisted on helping. While she slipped into the house to change, he headed to the barn and with Buddy's help, turned the horses out into the pasture so they could clean stalls.

"Fancy meeting you here."

She glanced at the door. Boots, his expression inscrutable, watched them.

"Good morning, Mr. Thomas."

"Stayed out a little late, Cassidy Anne."

She realized she'd dropped her gaze so that her guilt now appeared obvious—and that Boots had ignored Chance. She raised her chin and met the situation head-on—by ignoring the insinuation. "Chores are done. Any coffee left?"

"There is. But I figured y'all might be in need of something more substantial. Breakfast at the Four Corners. My treat."

She glanced at Chance, bemused by the expression on his face. He stared at Boots, but the smile curving his very sexy mouth looked almost hostile. She opened her mouth to decline and suggest that even she could scramble eggs, but her stomach growled. Loudly. Chance glanced at her and chuckled.

"Guess that means we're doing breakfast. I'll get washed up."

He disappeared into the tack room, taking longer than he needed so he could sort through his emotions. Boots Thomas didn't trust him, and Chance needed to figure out why. The old cowboy knew who he was. Did the man also suspect why he was pursuing Cassie? He stared at his reflection in the broken piece of mirror stuck up above the sink. Why *was* he after Cassie? He told his brothers and father it was business. But last night turned it into something else entirely.

Hell, he was falling for the girl. That was a big damn joke on him. Chance Barron didn't fall for girls. Life with the old man convinced him that love didn't exist. Lust? Oh, yeah. Lust was dependable. But love? With Cassidy Anne Morgan?

"Damn, son. You are in so much trouble now."

Over the sound of running water, he heard Cass leave. By the time he joined Boots to lean against the hood of his truck, she appeared on the porch, ready to go. Buddy lazed in the shade. Boots moved to the passenger side and as soon as he opened the back door, Buddy leaped into the backseat.

"No, Buddy. Get out." Looking mortified, Cass ran to the truck and did her best to pull the dog out. "You can't go."

"It's okay." He'd opened the driver's door and leaned in to watch.

"But Chance, those are leather seats."

"So?"

"So?" Her mouth gaped. "Let me at least get a blanket or something."

"He's fine, Cass. Just get in the truck. I'm hungry."

Her mouth gaped a little wider as she read his expression—and his double entendre. The tips of her ears burned as she flushed, and she ducked into the back before Boots got a good look at her. Buddy occupied the seat behind him, barking and looking pleased.

Once they got to the diner, he'd have to keep a low profile and hope no one recognized him. Clay, as a US Senator, was always in the limelight and Chase made the tabloids on a weekly basis. He supposed Chase's position as CEO of the entertainment and real estate arm of the family empire invited that sort of attention. Chance, along with Cord and Cash, did his best to stay out of the public eye. Maybe

he could pull this off. Even though he was senior partner
of his own law firm, he made sure his associates were the
ones on the news.

Cass hadn't been back to Four Corners since the day of
her dad's funeral. The warm pressure of Chance's palm
against the small of her back propelled her through the
door. A bell jangled merrily, and heads turned. Jovial greet-
ings rang out, and Boots stopped to visit with folks on the
way to a booth by the front window. Nadine appeared with
clunky ceramic mugs in one hand and a steaming coffeepot in the other.

Chance settled beside Cassidy and as soon as his thigh
brushed against her, it stayed. Moments later, a waitress
appeared with glasses of ice water, cutlery setups rolled
tightly in paper napkins and a metal pitcher of cream. Cass
doctored her coffee from the jug, watching the thick swirls
turn the rich sepia liquid in the mug to gentle café au lait.
They ordered. They ate. And she leaned into the corner listening to Boots and Chance. As the old man quizzed the
younger, she watched their expressions. Chance remained
relaxed, deflecting or answering the questions with good-
natured ease. Boots, cynical at first, relaxed, as well. She
could almost see the moment he made up his mind about
Chance.

Nadine returned frequently, perching beside Boots to
chat, her laughter filling the awkward moments. Cass
smiled but hid it behind her napkin. Nadine had a thing
for Uncle Boots, and if she knew him at all, he was rather
sweet on the woman, as well. To her knowledge, Boots
had never married and she wondered why now. Her smile
morphed into a yawn, despite the copious amounts of coffee she'd consumed.

"I think we need to get our girl home for a nap, Mr.
Thomas."

"Call me Boots, son."

Cass stared from one to the other, feeling as if an iceberg had just dislodged from a glacier. She would no longer have to justify Chance's presence or dating him. The idea left her feeling dizzy. *Were* they dating? Or had last night just been a one-night stand? He'd stayed to help in the barn today, and he certainly didn't seem in any hurry to leave. She wondered again what he did for a living. It paid well, whatever it was, based on his truck and his condo.

Both men made a grab for the check, but Chance snatched it first. He left cash to cover both bill and tip on the table and slid out, offering a hand to her. A bit shy, she placed her hand in his. Strong fingers closed around hers and with a gentle tug, he pulled her to her feet. He refused to relinquish her hand, and weaving through the diner to the door proved awkward. But she didn't care. Not one for public displays of affection, this particular PDA made her feel all warm and fuzzy inside. Outside, Buddy appeared from around the corner. He barked and jumped up on her, making her laugh.

"Bacon breath? You are so busted, dog!"

Boots climbed into the backseat with the dog, and she rode shotgun. Chance didn't seem the least bit embarrassed to hold her hand on the trip home, nor to kiss her in front of Boots once they arrived.

"I'll see you soon, darlin'." His words whispered in her ear after the kiss.

Cass resisted the urge to ask when that would be. Clingy and needy were not two adjectives she wanted added to her personal bio. Instead, she offered a wry smile. "You know where I live, cowboy."

Chance sprawled in the overstuffed leather chair, looking far more at ease than he felt. He could see the reflections of his brothers' faces in the highly polished surface of the mahogany conference table. His siblings ranged against him on the other side—all but one, and his face dominated the wide screen monitor on the wall. Chance studied them. Phones were ringing in Clay's office and he looked not only distracted but uncomfortable, as well. Of those arrayed on the other side of the table, Cord was the only one who would meet Chance's gaze directly. Chase had his smartphone out, thumbs flying as he texted or surfed the web or did something. Cash looked bored as he stared out the window over Chance's left shoulder.

"This feels an awful lot like an intervention."

"It doesn't have to be, Chance." As the oldest, Clay took the lead. He sighed, the sound not quite synced with his image. "I'm in the middle of the budget battle. I don't really have time for this petty squabble."

A burst of laughter erupted from Chase, and he paused in his texting. "You callin' the old man's squabble petty, Clay?"

"I am in this instance. Chance, you've stalled long enough. Just file the papers, foreclose on the place and get done with it."

"But you forget, Clay. There's a pretty girl involved. I think brother Chance is letting his little head think for him."

Chance glared at Chase and jumped in before his oldest brother could. "You're one to talk, bro. How many times have we bought *your* way out of woman trouble?"

With a negligent shrug, Chase focused once more on his phone. "Whatever. But I'm tired of these command performances. I'm in the middle of negotiations for a new resort property, and I damn sure don't need to be jetting back and forth."

Cash cleared his throat and sat up a little straighter. "Look, Chance, I know you like the girl. Hell, you've been with her almost every night since you got back from Chicago. I'm betting she's a pretty good—"

Before he realized what he was doing, Chance reached across the table and grabbed the front of Cash's shirt, his hand fisting in the folds of expensive Egyptian cotton. "Shut. Up. Cash. I know damn good and well you've been tracking me. That ends now. Today. You hear me? I'll handle this. In my own way and in my own time."

"No." The single word cut through the tense atmosphere. Cyrus Barron filled the doorway. "You will do this my way and in my time."

Chance released Cash and faced his father. The old man looked right through him. His heart pounded as anger surged up from his gut. "Why is this such a big deal?"

"It's a big deal because I say it is." Cyrus stalked the rest of the way into the room and stopped at the head of the table. He stared at his middle son, and his face twisted as if he'd stepped in manure. "That old bastard died before I could settle the debt between us so I'll settle it with his brat."

Wanting to pound his fists on the desk, or on his father's face, Chance clenched them at his sides and breathed instead. Forcing his anger down, he looked for the right argument. If the old man figured out Cass was important to him, all bets were off.

"Cassidy Morgan plans to sell the place and return to Chicago. She has a herd of cattle. Once they're sold, she can pay off her father's medical bills. We can buy the place from her with one offer and a certified check." He didn't back down from his father's glare.

Cyrus leaned over the table and jammed his finger into Chance's chest. It took every ounce of self-control to keep from breaking his father's finger.

"Ben Morgan double-crossed me and stole something important. I vowed then I'd ruin him. It may have taken me almost forty years, but by God I will have my revenge. Now sit down and shut up, Chancellor. You always were the runt of the litter." His father faced the monitor. "Clayton, you better have that damn Senate committee straightened out on the oil pipeline bill."

Chance sank onto his chair. Old taunts still hurt, but he wasn't that little boy anymore. He opened his mouth to continue the argument but snapped it shut as Cord delivered a shift kick to his shins under the conference table. He pressed his lips closed and glared at his father in silence.

"I've made a few phone calls," the old man continued. "That should take care of it. Don't screw it up, Clayton."

"No, sir. I won't."

Cyrus cast his gaze on his other sons and missed the grimace on Clay's face. Chance caught it, right before his father's eyes zeroed in on him again.

"As of now, Ben Morgan's brat will no longer have a way to get those cows to market." The cynical smile on his face spoke volumes. Chance braced for the other shoe to drop.

"We'll foreclose on the property, and she'll be left with nothing but a crapload of debt. Morgan's remaining medical bills are over fifty thousand dollars. We'll come in, sell off everything lock, stock and barrel and throw her and that old SOB Boots Thomas out on their asses."

Chance's gut roiled and he fought down a wave of nausea. What the hell was the old man doing? Cass had nothing to do with this ridiculous feud. His father was out to ruin a woman Chance cared about probably more than he should, given the circumstances. He bit his tongue and remained silent. He knew the old man too well, positive there was even more to come. His father pinned him with a cold stare.

"Quit stalling, Chance. I sent you to law school and let you start a law firm for a reason. Now get those papers filed. I want the foreclosure a done deal and everything liquidated." The old man's lips twisted into a parody of a smile. "Well, everything but Legend's Double Rainbow. That little stud colt will finally be mine, too." His father dismissed him with a negligent wave of his hand and turned his attention to the others. "Now, what the hell else have you morons managed to screw up?"

Chance tuned out the conversation, stewing in his own anger. He looked up to catch Cord studying him, his brother's expression both speculative and serious. He stared back. They were all chips off the old man's block and where Chance had once had some pride in that, now he wondered. Why the hell did he try so hard to win this man's respect? Forget love. Cyrus Barron only loved power and money. Yet Chance had spent his entire life trying to please the old bastard.

"Blood sticks together, boys. And you'd all better remember that. No one takes care of a Barron but another Barron. The rest of the world doesn't give a damn so why should we give a damn about them? Family is all that matters. You all clear on that?"

Silence reigned in the void left by the old man's departure. Even the phones in Clay's office had stopped ringing. Chase pushed his chair away from the conference table, stood and presented his backside to his brothers.

"Is there anything left?" He *whewed* dramatically as everyone chuckled. "Nice to know something's still there after that ass chewing." He turned back around and focused his gaze on Chance. "Do us all a favor. End this thing with the Morgan girl, get the job done and get the hell out of Dodge. There's not a woman alive who's worth the old man's wrath."

Chance remained still, staring at all of them in turn. "This doesn't bother any of you?"

Clay's exasperated voice issued from the monitor. "Since when did you go all noble, Chance? I don't have time for all this crap. Do your job." The monitor flickered to a blue screen.

Cash and Chase, like the twins they were, walked out

shoulder to shoulder without a word, leaving Chance and Cord at the table.

"What?" He glared at his older brother.

"Man, you have it bad." Cord shook his head from side to side, his expression solemn. "You really need to get over this girl."

"Why? Tell me why we have to destroy *her*?"

Cord leaned back in his chair and for a moment, Chance thought his brother would prop his boots up on the highly polished wood of the table. "Why not? It's what the old man wants. And what the old man wants—"

"The old man gets. Yeah, yeah. We've been saying that our entire lives, Cord. But what makes him right?"

Cord laughed, a deep, rolling laugh straight from the gut. "I never said the old bastard was right, Chance. But he is who he is. He's always run roughshod over anyone who got in his way. This time, it just happens to be a gal you have the hots for."

If looks could kill, as the old saying went, Chance's brother would have been BBQ. "Shut up, Cordell." He pushed to his feet and strode out the door, his brother's laughter following in his wake.

Nine

Chance chewed on the handful of antacids he'd just taken. Outside his office window, Oklahoma City spread out to the southwest like a crazy quilt of buildings, parks and river. Sunlight glinted off the fuselage of a plane lining up for a landing on a runway at Will Rogers International Airport.

The door opened behind him but he didn't turn until he heard a heavy body drop into one of the wingback chairs arranged in front of his desk.

"I don't really want to talk to you."

Cord tilted his head. "Fine. Don't talk. I just want you to listen anyway."

"Didn't you say enough downstairs?"

"No. I said what the old man wants to hear when he plays back the tapes of the meeting."

Chance pressed his palms on his desk and leaned forward. He glowered, hoping to cover up the despair he really felt. "Just toeing the family line then?" When Cord didn't reply, he sank into his desk chair. He closed his eyes and dragged the fingers of one hand through his once carefully combed hair. "Dammit."

"Is that all you have to say?"

"What do you want me to say, Cord? Let's trade places if you think this is so easy. Let me run the ranch and the oil company. You go to law school and do all this legal crap. You serve papers on a sweet little girl who's just trying to do the right thing. You sit in this chair and do the old man's dirty work."

"Wow. You might have a conscience after all."

Chance rolled his eyes. "Shut up, Jiminy Cricket."

Leaning back, Cord propped his booted feet on the desk. "Tell me about her."

"What's to tell?"

"Well, there must be something since she has you tied up in knots."

"She's sweet and funny and doesn't want to be a cowgirl."

"You forgot sexy, Chance."

"Yeah. She's that, too."

"I finally figured out how I know her."

Chance rocked forward, his eyes narrowed into a glare. "You know her?"

"Whoa, bro. Not in the biblical sense. Unlike you." Cord waggled his brows and laughed as Chance snarled. "Down, boy. That just confirms my suspicions. She was named the championship cowgirl at the Denver Stock Show the last year we competed. She looked mighty fine in tight jeans but way too young for me."

Closing his eyes, Chance leaned his head back and tried to relax. "When you called me in Chicago, I was trying to pick her up. I didn't know who she was then, Cord, not until I got home. She just wants to sell the place, pay off her father's debts and get on with her life." In Chicago. Without him.

"Damn, bubba. You have it even worse than I thought."

"Shut up."

"What are you going to do? If she finds out the old man is behind her troubles, she'll hate you."

"Is it too much to hope she doesn't find out? At least until I get her out of my system."

Cord rolled his eyes. "Get her out of your system? Yeah,

right. Like that's going to happen. You don't have a clue, Chance. She rode you hard, put you up wet and now she's got her spurs dug deep. If the circumstances were different, I might actually enjoy watching your fall from grace."

Chance raked his fingers through his hair again. "Our father is a real sonofabitch."

"Yeah. You got that right."

Cass stared at the pile of bills in front of her. She puffed out a breath and the straggle of hair hanging in her eyes danced. Picking up the checkbook, she sighed. No matter how many times she ran the numbers, there was way more owed than what was in the bank—even if she drained her savings account. She had to get those cattle sold, and she had to do it soon.

She called everyone on her father's list of cattle haulers. The answer remained the same.

"You're from the Crazy M? Sorry, we're booked solid."

"No, we don't have even one truck to spare."

"Sorry."

Everyone was sorry. Or not. But not one cattle hauler would accept a contract from her. She placed another call to the independent hauler her dad had used for years.

"I'm sorry, but I can't do a thing for you. It's a real shame, too. I thought the world of your dad."

"I can't believe that every trucking line in three states is busy hauling cattle."

The man on the other end of the phone line cleared his throat. The nervous sound made Cass wonder what was going on. "You don't have another contract, do you?" He cleared his throat again but didn't speak. "Why? If you thought so highly of my dad, why won't you haul the cattle for me?"

"It's not you, hon."

"Then what is it?"

"Not what. Who." She heard him take several deep breaths. "Look, I can't say anything more. I'm sorry. Things are what they are, and sometimes a workin' man has no choice. Please don't call me again."

The phone clicked and after a moment of dead air, a dial tone echoed in her ear. "Now what the heck was that all about?"

Boots looked up from his paper, the crinkles around his eyes looking sad. "I was afraid that's what was happenin'."

"What?" Her voice sounded sharper than she intended, but she was so frustrated she wanted to punch something. "Do you know what's going on, Uncle Boots?"

"It's a long story, honey, and I'm not positive, but I have a suspicion that a man by the name of Cyrus Barron has thrown a monkey wrench into things."

Everyone knew that name but she asked to be sure. "As in Barron Oil?"

"And Barron Land and Cattle Company."

"And Barron Entertainment?" Her voice squeaked a little.

"That would be him."

"But…why in the hell would he care about me hauling five hundred head of cattle to market?"

"I told you it's a long story, honey. There's somethin' maybe you need t'know about the Barrons…"

Before he could continue, Buddy jumped up and began barking madly. He hit the door and banged the unlatched screen open. A muffled voice greeted the dog and then boots on the wooden porch preceded a knock on the door.

"May I come in?"

Cassie's voice sounded resigned as she answered. "C'mon in, Chance."

He held the door and followed the dog inside. Her eyes looked bruised and something in his chest shifted. Chance glanced at the pile of papers in front of her before his gaze slid over to Boots. "Everything okay?"

"No."

Chance wanted nothing more than to take her in his arms. She looked so fragile...so *beaten*. "What's happened?"

Her frustration bubbled over. "I can't get anyone to transport my cattle to market."

He replied carefully. "It's spring. Everyone's shipping their feeder calves."

She shook her head, adamant when she added, "No. They don't have trucks available to *me*."

Chance cleared his throat and glanced away. "That doesn't...make sense."

"You haven't been talking to these people, listening to their lame excuses. I'm not paranoid." She thumped the table. "I've called everyone listed in Dad's files."

Cass blew out a huff of air that ruffled her bangs and slumped back the wooden chair. "I don't understand why. I mean...Dad had a great reputation. He always paid his bills. I can't even get the bank to call me back about the loan I told you about."

She snatched a handful of bills and waved them. "The hospital. His doctors. Even the funeral home. I can't pay anything until those cows sell. And if I can't get them to market, how the hell can I sell them?" Cassie looked so small and vulnerable Chance wanted to gather her into his arms. A tear spilled from her eye, and she scrubbed at her face, smearing it away. "And that's not the worst of it."

He gave up. Striding across the room, he pulled her into his arms and held her. "What else is going on?"

"I..." She shivered and he kissed her temple.

"It's okay, baby. I have you."

"My boss called. If I'm not back at my desk tomorrow morning, I'm fired. I have rent due on my place in Chicago, and bills, and I've spent almost everything in my checking account keeping things going here until I can get Daddy's estate settled."

Chance ground his back teeth together, anchoring his anger to keep it from spilling out. He wanted to hurt someone. His father. Her boss. Himself. He was every bit as guilty as anyone. When she pushed away, he dropped his arms.

"I'll be fine." Cass turned on her boot heel and marched to the door. "I need to get away for a while. I'm going for a ride." She held up her hand, palm facing them like a stop sign. "I'm going alone."

The screen door banged behind her, and Buddy nosed it. He looked back at the two men and whined. Chance walked over, opened the door far enough for the dog to slip through then let it close with a gentle bump. He watched the angry but broken woman stomp toward the barn and fought the urge to follow her, to take her into his arms and promise her that everything would be fine. As long as his father persisted in this vendetta, nothing would ever be fine for Cassidy Morgan. And now the other shoe had dropped.

"You know who's behind all this trouble with the cattle?"

Chance continued to stare out the door, refusing to look at Boots. "I have my suspicions."

"You gonna do anything about it, son? That little gal thinks the world of you, you know."

Would he? Could he? He'd spent his whole life in his father's shadow. As the family's attorney, he'd filed lawsuits and defended them, always putting Cyrus Barron and whatever Barron enterprise first. The old man was always right, and the whole world was wrong if they didn't agree.

Chance patted his pocket absently, hoping he'd slipped in the bottle of antacids. He hadn't.

Was Cord right? Was he finally developing a conscience? If so, it was a helluva time. He needed to be detached. Uninvolved. Cold. He'd meant to sleep with Cass, get her out of his system and walk away. But here he stood at the door of her house, watching her run away so she could cry alone. His father would crush her. And he could do nothing but stand by and watch.

"I have to go." He pushed open the door and stepped onto the porch.

"And here I thought maybe you'd grown a pair."

He couldn't even work up a smidge of righteous anger. The man was right. Cassidy Morgan had far more courage than he ever would.

"I'm sorry, Boots." He mumbled the words as he trudged down the steps. He didn't know if the other man heard him and didn't care either way. As he opened the door of his truck, he paused to watch Cass, riding the big sorrel bareback, charge out of the barn and race across the field toward a line of trees. What felt like a steel band constricted his chest, and his pulse hammered in his ears. Maybe he was having a heart attack. That would solve everything, so he almost hoped he was.

Chance climbed into the truck, knowing he was a coward. He glanced at the house where Boots stood in the doorway watching him. The best thing he could do was leave. Get out of Cassie's life. Do what he had to do. And then head to Vegas for a two-week binge of wild women, strong drink and lots of gambling. Except never seeing Cass again tore at his heart. The thought of touching another woman held no appeal. That left booze and poker, and he wasn't a big fan of either.

"I'm sorry, Cassidy Morgan. I'm sorry I'm not the man you deserve."

Ten

"No." Cass glared at the man sitting across from her in the booth at Nadine's diner.

"You aren't thinkin' this through, sugar."

"No, Boots. I can't take your money."

"Honey, your daddy was my best friend. He was more like my family than my own blood. And so are you. Family helps family."

Cass refused to look at his earnest face. Her untouched breakfast cooled on the plate as she drew desultory designs on the table from the condensation ring left by her ice water glass. "Sandra agreed to box up the stuff I want to keep and ship it, and then have a tag sale to dump the rest. I gave notice so I should get my apartment deposit back and the utility deposits will pay off the final bills I owe up there."

"You aren't going back to Chicago?"

She hated the hope she heard in his voice. She'd done a lot of thinking in the few days since her firing. She loved Chicago. Loved her job and her dinky apartment and the wind whistling off the lake so cold it could cut. She hated the heat and the dust and smells of living on the ranch. The dirty, back-breaking work. Didn't she?

"I can't afford it right now, Uncle Boots. Not until I get things settled here." She glanced up. "No. I'm still not going to take your money. You need it. Daddy wanted you to be comfortable. So do I."

"Honey, I don't need much. You're just as stubborn as Ben. Always gotta do it your own way."

She shrugged and dropped her gaze to the water doodles she'd made.

"What? My cookin' not good enough for you, Miz Cassidy Anne?" Nadine had appeared, coffeepot in hand, and her voice held not a lick of chiding. "You look like you lost your best friend, hon. You wanna tell ol' Auntie Nadine about it?"

Try as she might not to, she felt compelled to look up at the woman. Concern radiated in Nadine's expression even as the skin around her eyes crinkled from her friendly smile.

"Everything looks better with a full stomach and a cup of hot coffee."

"I don't think buttermilk pancakes will solve my problems, Nadine."

The woman shooed her over and plopped down on the booth's bench beside her. "But sometimes, talkin' things over with friends does. Boots told me a bit of what's goin' on. I'm sure sorry for your troubles. I know your daddy didn't figure on this crap happenin'. He was a planner, Ben Morgan was. Always one step ahead of life in his thoughts. We just need to do the same."

For a moment, anger welled up. How dare Boots discuss her business with a stranger! But then she saw the expression on his face, and things cleared up. Nadine wasn't a stranger. Not to Boots. He was sweet on the woman. And Nadine returned those feelings.

"Honey, your daddy had a passel of friends. He had an open hand when it came to helpin' folks. I'm sure they'd all step up to return the favor. You just need to figure out what it is you need."

"I need to get my friggin' herd to market." The words

erupted before she could think about them, her voice filled with all the anger and frustration she'd tamped down for a week.

A man at the counter swung around on his stool. "That's what cattle haulers are for."

Cass rolled her eyes. "Duh. But none of them will haul for me."

The man's brow furrowed, and he scratched his head, which set the John Deere cap on his head to dancing. "They locked you out?"

"Evidently."

"That don't seem fair."

She bit back another *duh*. "It is what it is. I still don't have a way to get the herd to market. If I use the old stock trailer at the ranch, I can only take a few at a time. Running them through the sale that way loses me money in the long run. I need a big ol' chunk of money to pay off everything." She didn't want to mention that she could barely afford gas for the truck.

Almost everyone in the diner turned to look at her, and she resisted the urge to bang her head on the table. A little boy perched on a stool at the counter continued to watch the TV above the cash register. An old black-and-white movie played across the screen. He tugged on his mother's sleeve and pointed at the screen. "Mommy, can I have cartoons?"

The young woman chuckled. "I can't believe you don't want to watch a cowboy movie, C.J. With John Wayne, no less."

The youngster offered a disgruntled expression and a deep sigh. "But...cartoons, Mom."

The man on the stool next to the boy winked. "Your mom's right, son. John Wayne and cattle on a trail drive is a classic Western story."

"Huh." The child scowled again before gazing at his mother impatiently.

Nadine slid out of the booth and headed for the remote control. "I think I can get the Cartoon Network, honey. Just give me a sec to find the right channel."

Cass twisted in her seat to stare at the TV before it flickered quickly through several channels and cartoons filled the screen. She shifted to stare at Boots. "No."

Boots looked perplexed as he returned her gaze. "No what?"

"I...nothing." She shook her head. "Just a really crazy idea. One that is way too far-fetched to ever work."

"I can see the wheels turnin', honey. Why don't you just tell me?"

She continued to shake her head, denying the wild scheme forming in her brain. "But..."

Nadine returned with a fresh pot of coffee and refilled their mugs. "Boots, you ever notice she gets that same look Ben got whenever he got a wild hair?"

"No. It's...there's no way. The idea is too ridiculous to even consider."

"Well, honey, if you don't tell us about it, there won't be a way 'cause we won't be able to help you figure out how to make it work." Boots sipped from his coffee mug.

Cass stared from one to the other. "A cattle drive." Nadine and Boots exchanged a cryptic look, and she sighed. "See? I told you it was ridiculous. There's no way we could do a trail drive from the ranch to the stockyards."

"Why not?"

Her jaw dropped. "Because, Uncle Boots. Half of Oklahoma City stands between the Crazy M and the stockyards. Not to mention a couple of major interstate highways."

"You know, that just might work." The man in the booth behind her tapped her on the shoulder. "You'd need some permits and stuff but you could move 'em along section line roads. Wouldn't have to touch many busy streets at all."

Were they not listening? She still wanted to bang her head on the table. This was too crazy to even contemplate.

"Anybody got a map?" Another man dragged a chair over and planted his beefy body at the end of the table. "We could draw out the route right now."

"No. Just…stop. It's just Boots and me. We can't handle five hundred head. And it's…what? At least twenty miles to the stockyards? We can't push cattle more than five maybe ten miles a day tops. There'd be no place to stop at night. No place to water them. I…thank you. All of you. But I…it won't work."

Her audience grumbled but turned away, returning to their own business. The idea was simply too preposterous to even consider. She drank her coffee, completely unaware it held neither cream nor sugar. There had to be another way. She just needed to figure out what it was. Maybe she'd call Chance. He'd disappeared after her outburst, but he'd called and left voice mails on her cell phone since then, asking how she was doing. He was a cowboy. And smart. Maybe he had some ideas that would help.

Late that afternoon, she clicked off the phone rather than leave yet another voice mail message for him. Boots was down at the barn working with the colt, and Buddy lay in a puddle of sunshine streaming through a window. He woofed, and his paws twitched as he chased something in his dreams. She dropped beside him on the floor and buried her fingers in his thick fur.

"Am I crazy, Buddy? I mean like totally insane? There's no way we can drive those cattle to the stockyards. The logistics alone are…I can't even wrap my brain around what would be involved. No. I can't do this. There's got to be another way. I'll go to the bank tomorrow and park myself outside the president's office until he meets with me." She nodded as if to punctuate her resolve. "He'll have to talk to me. Have to listen to me. And I'll work something out." Bending, she brushed her cheek across the top of the dog's head. "I have no choice, Buddy."

The dog whined and licked her chin. "I'm glad somebody still loves me."

"I'm glad somebody still loves me." Chance flashed his legal assistant a smile. "Thanks for staying late."

"I stay late every night. Say what you mean." She waggled her index finger at him, the other hand on her hip. "Why, thank you, Heidi, for taking all the heat from my family, for not making me talk to them."

She was right, but he sure hated to admit it. Even so, her attitude made him grin. "You are worth your weight in gold, Heidi."

"I'm getting that in writing so I can hold it over your head come bonus time." She leaned on his desk and closed the folder he'd been staring at for the past hour. "Shut it down, boss. Go home. Or go out. Go do something besides sit here and brood."

He kicked back in his desk chair and fiddled with the expensive pen in his hand. "You're on her side."

She laughed—long and hard. "Of course I'm on her side. Your father is an absolute alpha hotel."

Heidi's husband was retired military, and she tended to reduce terms used in the vernacular to their military equivalent. "Yeah. But what else is new?"

She stared at him, both hands on her hips now. "Really? You have to ask this question?" She rolled her eyes when he remained silent. "You, boss. You're what's new. The way you're looking at this situation, the way you're reacting.

This girl's gotten to you. Why her after all the other stuff your old man has done, I don't know. But you've changed."

He shook his head. "No. No, I haven't, Heidi. If I had, I wouldn't be sitting here with these papers on my desk."

Heidi snorted. "Yes, you have. The old Chance would have filed the paperwork the first day and served the girl at her daddy's funeral. The old Chance would not sit here stewing over what an alpha hotel his father is, and the old Chance would not care one whit that he was following in his old man's footsteps. But here you are." She shook her head and started to wag her finger one more time but resisted. "I'm going home. Turn out the lights when you leave, boss."

In the silence following her departure, Chance swiveled his chair to stare out the window behind his desk. The Barron Building, all forty stories of it, dominated the skyline. From his view on the thirty-sixth floor, the southwestern expanses of the metroplex unfolded before him. He picked out the historic Farmer's Market building and beyond it, Stockyard City. The phone on his desk rang, but he ignored it. It was still ringing when his cell phone started. He didn't have to check his caller ID. At least one brother would be calling, probably two. Or worse, Cassie's number would stare back at him.

He'd done what they wanted—distanced himself from her. He listened to her messages—for a while at least—craving some tiny connection to her. Then he had to delete them without listening. Her voice tore his heart to shreds, and it took every ounce of self-discipline to keep from driving to the Crazy M to claim her.

Why did he have to choose between his family and the wonderful woman who'd captured his heart? But he knew the answer whenever he looked in the mirror. Take away everything else, he was a Barron. Through and through. Dammit. And when it came to women, being a Barron guaranteed the lady in question would get hurt.

* * *

Cass wore the same austere suit she'd worn to her dad's funeral. The sleeves bunched a little, and she realized all the physical labor she'd done lately had changed her body—slimmed some of the curves and packed on muscle. That wasn't a bad thing.

An office door opened, and she sat up straighter, but the woman who emerged ignored her, walking straight to the front of the bank.

Cass settled back against the uncomfortable chair and wondered again why she was doing this. She hated the ranch. The life didn't suit her at all. She wanted to sleep late on the weekends. Go out to dinner. Work in an office where her friends gossiped about the latest celebrity breakups and makeups, the hot new television show, the ugly dresses on the red carpet. Except she didn't care about those things. Not really.

Another door opened and she leaned forward, peering down the long hallway. A man stepped out and headed away from her. She glanced at the wall clock above the receptionist's head. Eleven o'clock. Two hours she'd waited. So far. The loan officer had already passed her up the chain to the bank president—who was stalling her. Surely he would leave for lunch. If she couldn't get in to see him before, she'd grab him on his way out.

At 12:15, a pizza delivery guy showed up with eight boxes. Pepperoni. Onions. Tomato sauce and baked cheese. The scents blended together, and her stomach growled. Offices emptied, the occupants all rushing down the hall to what she figured was a conference room. A security guard arrived and sat at the receptionist's desk. He glowered at her from time to time.

At four, she was thirsty, hungry, in desperate need of the restroom, but unwilling to give up. The man had to go home sometime. The phone on the desk buzzed, and the girl picked it up.

"Yessir... No, sir. Hasn't moved... Sitting here all day... Yessir." The receptionist covered up the speaker end of the receiver. "Mr. Leonard can't see you today. You might as well go home."

"I'll stay in case he has a cancellation in his schedule. And I'll just be back tomorrow. Tell him I'm not going away."

The girl sighed dramatically, swiveled her chair so that her back was turned and whispered into the phone. A door at the very far end of the hall opened. "Mr. Leonard can give you ten minutes. But that's all."

Cass jumped to her feet and all but jogged down the hall. Leonard sat behind his desk looking distinctly uncomfortable. He'd rolled his sleeves down but they looked rumpled, and he'd made no pretense at straightening his tie. His florid face glistened with a sheen of sweat despite the cold air venting from the overworked air conditioner.

"I can't help you," he began without preamble.

"How do you know? I haven't asked for anything."

"I know what you want, Miss Morgan. Your father owes this bank two hundred and fifty thousand dollars, give or take some interest. Are you prepared to pay that amount today?"

"I can't. I need an extension."

"The matter has been referred to legal counsel for collection and foreclosure on the assets and is no longer my responsibility."

She'd been ready to launch into her argument when the import of his statement sank in. "Wait... What? Foreclosure? But the papers—"

"Ms. Morgan, loan payments were deferred to a balloon payment at the end of the loan period. If you are prepared to pay the full amount due and owing, the bank will halt the collection proceedings. If you aren't, then the matter is out of my hands."

"You can't just do things like this."

"I not only can, young lady, but it's done. This bank is not in the habit of buying cattle, and that is essentially what we would have to do since your father defaulted on the loan." He leaned back and rocked, his fingers laced across his ample belly. "I work for the bank. The loan is in default. Filing suit was the financially sound action for this institution. The matter is out of my hands."

"But…" She sat, stunned and speechless.

"Your time is up. You need to leave, Miss Morgan, or I will call security and have you removed."

"But…"

He leaned forward and tapped a button on his phone. "Call security to my office."

Cass glared at the man but rose from the chair. "My daddy trusted you."

She spun on her heel and marched out with her head held high, brushing by the startled guard. He shadowed her all the way to the parking lot and waited until she climbed into Boots's beat-up old truck, started it and drove out of the parking lot.

"So much for the friendliness of small-town banks," she groused.

At the next stoplight, she dug her cell phone out of her purse and dialed. The incessant ring echoed from the speaker. "C'mon, Chance. Pick up. Please…"

"You have reached my voice mail. You know what to do."

Yeah, she knew what to do. Why the hell was she depending on the jerk anyway? He sweet-talked her, wined her, dined her and jumped her in bed and then he no longer had time for her. Well, fine. She didn't need him. She didn't need anybody.

A horn honked and startled her out of her thoughts. She focused on driving until she got to a little place next to the highway. It wasn't the Four Corners but the scent of BBQ wafting through the truck's open window made her drool and her stomach gnaw on itself.

Inside, the wooden-planked walls looked grimy and smoke-stained, but the food still smelled heavenly. Antiques and old pictures littered every surface. She ordered ribs and fries, heaped her plate with onions, dill pickle chips and jalapeños, and sat down at a little table in the corner.

She bit into the first rib and almost moaned. Plastic squeeze bottles held different sauces and ketchup. Experimenting with the various flavors, she found a mix she liked, dragged the rib through the puddle of sauce on her plate and devoured it.

As she finished off the last of the homemade apple cobbler and ice cream, Cass realized this would be the last time she splurged. She had less than a thousand dollars in her checking account. The ranch account had enough to pay the bill at the electric co-op. The propane company had told her they could wait, and she had almost a full tank at the house anyway.

No job. No income. The loan was due, and she had no clue how to pay it. A headache formed between her eyes, and she rubbed her forehead. Why did she even care? She hated the ranch. Didn't she? Hated Oklahoma. But not a certain man who lived here.

She could just walk away. Not look back. Leave Boots and Buddy and—she nipped that thought. She did not want to think about Chance. About leaving him. Her life was in Chicago. Not here. Wasn't it? She didn't want to deal with the tangle of emotions Chance conjured up. Why hadn't he returned her calls?

People gave up and walked away all the time. But she wasn't a quitter. Her daddy would be spinning in his grave—or in that little box holding his ashes—if he could hear her thoughts.

I don't raise quitters, honey. You wipe those tears, get back in that saddle and ride. You're a Morgan. Show 'em what you're made of.

"Oh, Daddy," she murmured. "I miss you. What am I going to do?"

Something clattered back in the kitchen, and she jerked her head at the sound. Broken glass and spilled food. Yeah, that was a terrific sign from heaven. She glanced out the window but a photo beneath it caught her attention. Faded with age, it showed a group of cowboys on horseback. A herd of cattle milled behind the riders. Leaning closer, she peered at the legend on the photo. *1944—Calvin Barron and hands deliver herd to Oklahoma City National Stockyards.*

"That was quite a day."

Cass jumped and jerked her head around. An old black man in a stained apron chuckled. "The war was on and gasoline was bein' rationed. Old Mr. Barron, he had him a herd of prime cows and no way to get 'em to market. The gov'ment wanted them heifers to feed the army, but them ol' boys had to figure out a way to get 'em to the stockyards to put 'em on the train."

Dizzy as ideas whirled in her head, Cass felt as if she was on the verge of discovering something important. Then the name clicked. "Wait. *Old* Mr. Barron?"

"Yes, ma'am. Mister Cal was the current Mr. Barron's daddy. Mr. Cal was sure anxious t'get those cows to the railhead. Story goes they were all sittin' around drinkin', and those boys decided they'd have an old-fashioned trail drive. So they did. Took 'em nigh on two weeks but we pushed that herd from Mr. Barron's ranch up on the North Canadian River and right down into the stockyards. The newspaper came out and took pictures. Some radio guy from back East came out to interview folks."

Cass glanced at him. "Wait... You said *we*? You rode with them?" She leaned closer to the picture, studying it.

He tapped the back corner, and she squinted at the grainy photo. She could just make out a chuck wagon in the background. A man with dark skin stood beside it while a little boy waved from the wagon's seat.

"My pop was the chuck wagon cook, and I got t'tag along. That was quite an adventure for a kid like me."

She smiled and resisted the urge to kiss his cheek. "Thank you."

The crinkles smoothed from his face as his expression turned curious. "For what?"

"For your excellent BBQ. For coming out here to talk to me. For...for giving me the faith that maybe I can do what needs to be done. I gotta go!"

She dashed out to the old truck, climbed in and pulled out her phone. Cass stared at it, gulping in long breaths as she attempted to quell her excitement. "Daddy, we might just be able to pull this off. With a lot of help." She'd give Chance one more...chance. She chuckled at the irony, but was barely able to breathe around the anticipation. When she got his voice mail, she didn't care. Her enthusiasm bubbled over as she left a garbled message, not even aware when it clicked off automatically.

Eleven

Chance's fingers curled into fists as he stared at his phone. He'd resisted the urge to answer, but had to listen to this voice mail, had to hear her voice. The message…hurt. She burbled with excitement, the words rushing like a stream tumbling over rocks.

"Saw the banker finally. Sorry sonofagun. He said the bank's foreclosing, Chance. But it doesn't matter. I can get the cattle to the stockyards. I know I can. You won't believe what happened. You know Cyrus Barron? Jeez, that man has more money than Midas. Anyway, I found out something tonight. You won't believe this. His father did a cattle drive. In the forties. During the war. I can—" The phone cut off.

He couldn't breathe. His chest felt like a boa constrictor had wrapped around him, squeezing all the air out. For a minute, he thought she'd found out about his father. When she continued babbling and her excitement level ratcheted up a notch, he'd tried to listen but the pounding blood in his ears muted any sound. He hit the replay button and listened again, prepared this time.

Cattle drive? During the war? What the hell was she talking about? And more important, what relevance did it have now? He grabbed his phone and hit a speed dial number.

"Oh? So now you decide to talk to me?"

"Shut up, Cord. She knows the bank is foreclosing."

"Does she know why?"

"I don't think so."

"You don't *think* so?"

"I don't know, Cord, and I really don't care. She called, really excited, and the way she said the old man's name, I don't think she knows. But I need some information."

"About what?"

"About some cockamamie idea she got from somewhere. Do you know anything about a Barron cattle drive?"

"Dude, seriously? The old man pushing cows?"

He heard the clacking of a computer keyboard. "No, not the old man, Granddad Cal. In the forties, during the war."

"Huh. Color me impressed. There's a big file on it in the *Oklahoma Chronicle*'s morgue. Hang on a sec and I'll forward it to you. To make a long story short, Granddad Cal had a crapload of cows to sell and because of gas rationing, he decided to herd them from the ranch to the stockyards. The thing got a lot of attention. According to the file, it was even featured in a newsreel at the movies. The last cowboy. That sort of thing. Bottom line, he got the herd to market and made a killing. Army paid top dollar. Drove those steers straight into box cars and shipped 'em off to Chicago for slaughter. Why? What's this got to do with the Morgan situation?"

Chance stared out the window wondering the same thing. "I don't know. Yet. I'll keep you posted."

"Nice to have you back on board, bro. Now get the paperwork finished. The old man wants the notice of foreclosure served pronto."

His brother's words echoed in his head. *Nice to have you back on board.* But was he? He needed to see Cassidy. Find out what harebrained stunt she was planning. And then he'd talk her out of it. He'd make a few calls. Get her another job in Chicago. His heart hammered at the thought. Was that what he wanted?

It would be the simplest solution. She'd go back to Chicago. Their relationship, if it could be called that, would be over. She would no longer be a burr under his saddle, and she'd never know that his family—that *he*—had betrayed her. There was only one problem with that plan. He didn't want her to go. He wanted her to stay. And he wanted her to care about him. Like he cared about her. There. He admitted it. He cared about Cassidy Morgan. He shouldn't. Didn't want to. But he did. No matter how many calls he ignored, how far away from her he stayed, his heart betrayed him. He was a coward, despite the fact he loved her. Admitting it to himself should make him feel better. It didn't. He felt like the biggest bastard on the planet. She deserved a better man, a man worthy of her.

"Dammit all to hell. How did my life get so complicated?"

Staring at the open folder on his desk, he sighed. Family was everything. Blood was thicker than water. All the clichés his father hammered into his sons as they grew up in his shadow came back to haunt him. He wanted to do the right thing. But what was it?

Boots stumbled out of his room and headed straight for the coffeepot. Nosy, Cass watched him. He walked back to the table and peered curiously at the maps. "You look a little peaked this morning, Uncle Boots. Bad night?"

He muttered something under his breath and she thought she caught the words, "honky tonk," "dancing," and "that fool woman."

She bit her lip to hide a smile. "Yeah…gotcha. None of my business. I suggest we institute a don't-ask, don't-tell policy around here when it comes to our social lives."

He growled and sipped his coffee. Then he tapped a finger on the map. "You planning a trip?"

Cass pushed back from the table, snagged her own mug and took a sip. She grimaced but swallowed the cold coffee. She headed to the sink to dump the contents and pour a fresh cup. "Sort of." She returned to the table, sat and gestured for Boots to join her. "We need to talk."

"No luck with the banker, I take it?"

"None. The bank is foreclosing unless I pay off the loan on or before the due date.''"

He stared at her a full minute, his expression never changing before he asked, "You gonna explain the maps?"

She inhaled and rushed on. "For the cattle drive. It's been done before. Granted, it was almost seventy years ago but Calvin Barron…" She would have missed his expression if she hadn't been so intent on watching him. "What?"

"Nothing. Go on."

She knit her brows, puzzling through his reaction but continued doggedly. "I'll need permits. I plan on going to the commissioners of Canadian and Oklahoma Counties today to find out. Unless you need the truck?" She batted her eyes at him. "You know, to go to the Four Corners or…something."

He muttered under his breath, and she had to choke back a laugh as he blushed beneath his tan. "Take the damn truck. I have fence to ride." He pushed back from the table, the chair legs scraping against the scarred linoleum.

Cass paused to throw her arms around the old man's neck as he sat in his recliner. "This is going to work, Uncle Boots. I just know it!" The only damper on her enthusiasm was the fact Chance still hadn't called her. She alternated between concern and anger. If he'd blown her off, he could have been man enough to say so instead of keeping her dangling. But she was enough of a worrywart to wonder if something bad had happened to him. "Maybe Chance will help out, too."

"I hope so, baby girl." He muttered something under his breath that sounded like "for your sake."

Cassie kissed the top of his head, wondering at his words. Chance would call. She argued with herself, ending with the final insistent word as she muttered, too. "He will."

The next afternoon, Cass rode toward the barn, Buddy trotting beside her horse. Her sleeve was torn, and a few bloodstains spotted the frayed fabric. She'd stretched a strand of barbed wire too taut, and it had wrapped around her arm when it snapped. She'd have to make a trip to a clinic to get a tetanus shot. Her last booster was long out of date. Hot, sweaty and physically worn out, she wasn't looking forward to trekking into town.

As she neared the metal structure, something moved inside, and Buddy took off at a run. His excited barking reached her, and she nudged Red into a trot. Her heart skipped a beat when she recognized the man who stepped into the sunlight. Chance. She'd all but given up on him. He hadn't returned any of her calls. Her traitorous heart galloped at the sight of him, a stupid grin spread across her face and she laughed like a giddy girl on her first date.

He shaded his eyes and raised his hand in a rather tentative wave. She resisted the urge to wave madly back at him as she reined Red to a walk and then stopped the big horse several yards away. After dismounting, she did her best to ignore her emotions and the man creating havoc with her pulse rate.

"Gee, fancy meeting you here." She was so proud of herself. Just a hint of sarcasm and no breathy sigh.

He stepped closer and reached out, but she wasn't sure whether he meant to touch her or take the reins. "Cass, we should—what the hell?" He grabbed her arm, his hand gentle despite the urgency in his grip. "What happened?"

She tugged her arm, but his fingers didn't relinquish their hold. "I had a fight with a string of barbed wire. I won."

"Well, it doesn't look that way to me. You're bleeding."

"No, I'm not. It's dried. Mostly."

"We need to get you to the ER."

"No, *we* don't. In case you've forgotten in your rather noticeable absence, I was fired. That means no more insurance. That means I can't pay an ER bill."

"When was your last tetanus shot?"

"Long enough ago that I need one. But not at the ER. I can't afford five hundred dollars for a stupid shot. One of the drugstores in town has a clinic. I can get a booster there."

"Get up to the house and clean out the wounds. I'll put Red up and then come help."

She blew out a breath and her bangs, even though they were sweat-damp, danced from the force. "I'm a big girl, Chance. I can doctor myself and drive to the clinic."

"Driving what? The tractor?"

She leaned around him and glanced through the barn. Boots's pickup was gone. "Oh…"

"You. House. Now. I'll be up after I take care of Red, and we'll go to the clinic." He held up his hand, palm facing her. "No arguments."

Huffing and muttering under her breath about his bossiness, she relinquished the reins and marched through the barn. Buddy trotted beside her until she arrived at the far door; then the dog abandoned her to go back to Chance. "Traitor."

Two hours later, her arm properly bandaged and sore from the injection, Cass sat in a booth across from Chance at the Four Corners. A mound of mashed potatoes smoth-

ered in cream gravy perched next to a chicken-fried steak.
Fried okra and more gravy appeared in separate bowls on
the girl's next trip.

"Do I need to cut up your meat?"

She jerked her chin up and glared across the table. "I'm
not helpless, Chance. I am perfectly capable of cutting up
my own chicken fry." To prove her point, she grabbed the
knife and fork and proceeded to carve off a bite. She even
managed to hide her grimace when her upper arm throbbed
with pain from the action.

They ate in silence, though Chance watched her every
move. Self-conscious, she took little bites and made sure
her mouth stayed closed as she chewed. As the waitress
cleared her plate, she met his gaze.

"What?"

"Hmmm?" He seemed distracted, his eyes watching
her mouth.

"I guess you've been really busy. Or something?" Her
inner skeptic was back, front and center. Then an emotion
she couldn't decipher slid across his face before he shuttered his expression. She never wanted to play poker with
this man. He reached across the table and covered her hand
with his. She did her best to ignore the frisson of desire
ignited by his touch. As much as she wanted to stay angry
with him, she melted inside whenever he looked at her.

"You can't be serious, Cass."

Confused, she stared at him. "Serious? About what?"

He nodded toward the cash register and the bulletin
board hanging on the wall beside it. "A cattle drive. Really?"

She swiveled in the booth to see. Sure enough, her flier
asking for volunteer drovers was displayed in front of them.
Turning back to Chance, she readied for battle. Here she'd
been all "ooey-gooey" about being with him again and now
this? The dismissive tone of his voice set her off.

"How else can I get the herd to the stockyards? I can't hire a hauler. I talked to the sale manager. He said if I don't bring them all in at once I'll lose major money. And frankly? At this point, I can't afford to lose another dime."

She combed frustrated fingers through her bangs, wincing as she flexed her biceps. So much for him understanding and wanting to help. "I'm out of time, Chance, which you'd know if you ever listened to your voice mail." She watched as the arrogant facade he'd worn crumbled a bit. Maybe she could play poker with him after all. Score one for her.

"I've been busy, Cass. I'm…sorry."

A snort erupted—half bitter laugh, half the sound of derision it was meant to be. "Busy? Well, guess what, cowboy. Me, too. I'm hanging on by my fingernails. I'm stuck with a ranch I never wanted in the first place but all my options were ripped out from under me. I have no choice. I walk away with nothing after a forced liquidation sale, declare bankruptcy and hope to hell I can live in the homeless shelter until I can find a job."

He opened his mouth to protest, but she cut him off. "I don't own a car, Chance, so I can't live in it. Nadine has been after Boots forever. If he has any sense, he'll marry her and move in with her, and take Buddy, Red and Lucky with him. My other option is to stay and fight. I'm not paranoid, but I'm really starting to wonder. The bank decides to foreclose. There's not a cattle hauler in three states that'll talk to me. I lose my job." She ticked off the points on her fingers.

"The market is prime right now, and I've got Grade A beef on the hoof, grass-fed and tender. Daddy gambled everything on that herd. I can't let him down. I can't turn tail and run, as much as I'd like to just find a hole, crawl into it and die. I wasn't raised that way."

She paused for a breath, struck silent for a moment by

Chance's expression. A mixture of admiration, sadness and something she didn't want to identify but hoped like hell wasn't guilt etched the handsome planes of his face. He met her gaze, but he blinked first.

His hand captured one of hers again while the other cupped her cheek. "Dammit, Cassie. I…care about you. I don't want you to get hurt."

"Too late for that." He winced at her cutting tone, but she didn't care. Much. Tired of feeling alone, she leaned into his palm. "Help me, Chance. Help me make everything right again."

His expression softened, and his fingertips caressed her skin but he didn't say anything as he dropped his hand.

Exasperated, she pulled away from him. "You can help me or get the hell out of my way, Chance." When he remained silent, she shrugged. "Fine. Thanks for dinner, but I need to get home. I've got a lot of work to do to get ready for the trail drive."

The uncomfortable trip home couldn't end fast enough. Cass had the passenger door open before Chance put the truck in Park. She hopped out, slammed the door and trotted toward the barn, hoping he'd get the hint and just leave. She still had evening chores to finish.

Aware that Chance had cut the motor on the pickup and now followed her, she did her best to ignore him. Every time she thought their relationship held some promise, he dashed cold water on the whole idea by his actions. Fine. She could deal with that. By not dealing with him. She wouldn't think about him, wouldn't plan on him ever being a part of her future. She could stand on her own two feet, and she would.

Cass climbed up to the loft and dragged a bale of alfalfa hay to the edge. She shoved it over and waited a heartbeat before calling out, "Heads up." She snickered when Chance stumbled backward out of the way.

Back on the main floor, she snagged a pair of wire cut-

ters and snipped the baling wire. After splitting the bale
into blocks, she grabbed an armful and paced the length of
the barn, putting hay into the mangers of each stall. When
she got to the colt's stall, she glanced in. He lay on his side
and didn't raise his head as she clucked to him.

"Doc?" He still didn't respond so she whistled sharply.
The horse merely flicked an ear. She fumbled with the
latch, frantic to get into the stall to check on him.

"Cass? What's wrong?" Chance covered her hands with
his and stilled them. "Here. I'll do it."

A moment later, he had the door open, and she rushed
in. Doc's legs had brushed back and forth so hard, the horse
had cleared the straw down to the dirt floor. She dropped
to her knees and stroked his neck. Running a hand across
his withers and then his belly, she stilled. This was bad.
Really bad. His belly felt hard and looked bloated.

"We need to get him up on his feet." She stood and
bent over, tugging on Doc's halter but nothing happened.
"Chance, help me!" Her voice broke, revealing her help-
lessness.

"Easy, baby. Calm down. Let me get a look."

She backed away, but hovered close. "What's wrong
with him?" Her stomach tightened and the fried food from
dinner was a queasy lump threatening to choke her. She
swallowed then shoved her hands in her pockets to keep
from wringing them.

"I think it's colic, Cass, and he doesn't look good. I'm
going to call the vet."

She shook her head. "Oh damndamndamn. I...I don't
think you can get one to come. I can't pay."

"It's okay, Cass. We'll figure it out. Stay here with him.
I'll make a couple of calls."

Chance backed out of the stall as she knelt in the hay,
petting the colt and crooning softly. She seemed oblivious
to him. Even so, he stepped outside the barn before he di-

aled the first number. As soon as he had the information he needed from his brother, he ended the call before Cord could launch into all the reasons his presence at the Crazy M was a bad idea.

Besides, he had a good reason—one even his father might applaud, given the old man wanted the colt for his own. If Doc died, no one would profit. He kept telling himself that's why he was dialing the emergency large animal vet. He gave his full name, directions and a description of the colt's symptoms. He also guaranteed payment.

He'd just finished the call when Boots arrived. Chance squared his shoulders and prepared to do battle with the other man. He didn't have to wait long for Boots to fire the first shot.

"What are you doing here?"

"Cass got hurt." He held up his hand. "It's not serious. She got caught in some barbed wire and needed a ride so she could get a tetanus shot. But when we got back, she found the colt down in his stall. I've called the vet." Boots glared at him, and Chance worked to remain calm.

"You haven't answered my question. Why are you here?"

Why *was* he here? Because he couldn't stay away from her? Because she had rubbed a raw spot right over his heart? He gave the only answer he had. "I don't know, Boots. There's something about her. Something special. I just can't stay away."

"Your daddy is behind all her troubles, ain't he."

As Chance had suspected, Boots knew the truth. Since the man hadn't asked a question, no answer was required.

"You gonna let him get away with this? With hurtin' her like he's doin'?"

Chance glanced over his shoulder and lowered his voice. He wasn't ready for Cass to discover the truth. Not yet. Not until he had an opportunity to explain things to her.

"There's nothing I can do, Boots. The old man holds all the cards in this game."

"Game? This is a game to you?"

He shook his head, adamant in his denial. "No. That's not what I meant. Dammit. Have you ever known Cyrus Barron to lose at anything?" Boots stared at him and, while it took some effort, Chance steadily returned the man's gaze.

"Yeah. I have. Her name was Colleen. A damn finer man wooed that woman, married her and produced that little girl in there."

"Uncle Boots!" Cass's panicked shout cut off any retort Chance might have made. He beat the older man to the stall by a few strides, then waited in the doorway while Boots eased through and knelt beside her.

"It's gonna be okay, baby girl. Chance called the emergency vet."

"How can we pay, Uncle Boots? The vet'll put him down instead of treating him if we can't pay."

Her anguish slammed into Chance's chest. "I'll take care of it, Cass. Don't worry."

"You? How can you afford it? This could cost thousands of dollars."

He bit back his first answer—that he had a credit card with no limit. Hell, he had a sports car sitting in his garage that cost as much as some people's houses. He'd always worked, but he'd never had to worry about getting paid, or having to save up money to buy something, or pay a bill.

"I have it covered, Cass. I promise." He recognized the argument she started to raise by the look on her face. "And we'll work out a way for you to pay me back. Not charity. A loan. Okay? Right now, let's just get the little guy fixed."

Boots had a stubborn look on his face—one Cass was extremely familiar with—but he didn't say anything. After a staring match with Chance, Boots turned his gaze to her. "I'm goin' up to the house to get a few things. I'll be back before the vet gets here." The look he leveled at Chance as he backed out of the stall spoke volumes. Problem was, Cass couldn't translate it.

"Do the right thing, son."

And what the heck did Boots mean by that parting shot? Wrung out emotionally and on edge already, she waited until she heard the barn door close before she broached the subject. "What's he talking about, Chance?"

With a weary sigh, he squatted in the straw across from her and took his own sweet time getting settled with his back against the wall. "It's a long story. And it doesn't really matter right now anyway."

She stared at him from under furrowed brows. "I've got nothing but time at the moment."

Buddy lay down beside Chance and rested his chin on the man's thigh. The dog closed his eyes as Chance ruffled his ears.

"Traitor." She muttered the word but both dog and man seemed to chuckle at her. "Why did you come back tonight?"

"I didn't come *back*. I just…I never left, Cass. Not in the sense you mean. I have a job. I have bills to pay, too."

Heat flushed her face. "I will pay you back."

Chance shook his head. "That's not what I meant. I have the vet bill covered."

She tilted her head. "Why doesn't Boots trust you?"

He wouldn't look at her. "He has his reasons."

"What are they?"

"Look, I don't really want to get into it right now, okay?"

She blinked, taken aback by the vehemence in his voice. Even Buddy raised his head to stare up at the man. "Well, I do. Maybe I shouldn't trust you, either."

"Maybe you shouldn't."

His muttered admission shocked her, even as his stony expression revealed nothing and completely shuttered any emotions he might be feeling.

"Fine. Just…fine."

She continued to stroke the colt's neck and shoulder. Two could play that game, so she steadfastly ignored Chance. The problem with ignoring him, though, was that it left her mind free to wonder. Boots wasn't a suspicious man by nature, but he was a smart man and a good judge of both horses and men. He clearly did not like Chance. Hadn't almost from the first, truth be told. Come to think of it, she'd been leery of him, too, that first time he showed up unannounced and knew all about the colt.

The longer she stewed about the situation, the more suspicious she became. Chance had emerged from the barn when she rode up. How long had he been there? Had he done something to Doc? He'd been pretty dang insistent she go to the ER, which would have taken hours. After she'd insisted on going to the minor care clinic, he'd persisted until she agreed to dinner. Had he done that to stall her? Was he buying time so she'd come home to a dead colt? Had he poisoned Doc? And then called in his own vet? So the vet could finish the job…or fix the colt so Chance didn't get caught?

She pushed to a sitting position and stared at Chance. He leaned against the wall, his legs sprawled in front of him, eyes closed. But she seriously doubted he was asleep.

"What did you do to him?"

Chance didn't bother to open his eyes. "I didn't do a damned thing."

"You were in the barn, Chance. Alone. And he was fine when I left to mend the fence." He opened his eyes and leveled a look at her that might have chilled her to the bone if she hadn't been so full of righteous anger.

She kept pushing. "You show up here all solicitous and

kind and wanting to help. Who the hell are you, Chance? Why do you care? You obviously have money. You drive a brand-new truck. You live in that fancy condo down in Bricktown. Hell, I don't even know what you do for a living. You aren't a cowboy. As much as you might pretend to be, you aren't."

"I'm a lawyer."

That stopped her cold, her mouth hanging open just as she was about to start a new tirade. She snapped her jaw closed and stared at him in consternation. "A lawyer?"

He shrugged. "I've been a cowboy, too. I used to rodeo. A long time ago."

Something about his expression triggered a memory, but she shoved it aside. "So what? You play at being a cowboy now? And how did you know my dad? Why were you at his funeral?"

"I was there to see you."

That shocked her silly. "Me?" Her voice squeaked, and she swallowed around the frog in her throat. The colt stirred, as if he sensed her upset, so she roped in her emotions. After several deep breaths, she continued, her voice calm now. "I'd never met you before Chicago. Why were you looking for me?"

"I...just was."

She grimaced. "That's certainly cryptic. Can you be a little more specific?"

"No. The reason doesn't matter. But *this* does. Do you really believe I would hurt the colt? Hurt any animal?" His face remained expressionless but for a narrowing of his eyes and a slight jut of his chin. His voice sounded cold, and she decided right then she never wanted to be on the wrong side of the courtroom from him.

"I don't get you, Chance. I don't know why you're here. I...jeez. We've had some good times. Sex. Granted, the sex was fantastic but—"

"But what? We didn't have sex, Cassie. I made love to you. I..." He choked off whatever he was going to say but stayed on the offensive. "Is that all you can manage? Just sex? What's your deal? Relationships too sticky for you?"

She rocked back from the anger in his voice. "Whoa, dude. Back right the hell up. You're the one who didn't return my calls."

"I couldn't."

"Couldn't? What? You flushed your phone down the toilet? Your dog ate it? Oh, wait, you don't have a dog." She glared at Buddy. "You just steal mine."

"There are...extenuating circumstances." He clenched his jaw, and the words gritted out between lips stretched tight across his teeth.

"Extenuating circumstances? What's that? Legalese for I can't be bothered?"

Chance rubbed his temple, eyes closed. When he spoke, he seemed to have leashed his temper. "That's not fair, Cass. You have no idea what's going on. What's at stake."

She wanted to throw her hands up in the air and scream but Doc was restless again. She bridled her emotions though her angry response hissed out. "How the hell am I supposed to know if you don't tell me!"

He ground his teeth together. "I can't tell you. Not right now." He dragged the fingers of one hand through his hair and sighed. His gaze caught and held hers. "Please. Can you just trust me? For a little while longer?"

So many replies popped into her head. *Why should I? How can you ask that? Oh, hell no!* But as she looked at his face, recognized the pleading for understanding in his eyes, the grim set of his mouth, which all showed a crack in the emotions he did his best to stonewall deep inside, none of those admonitions worked. Between one thudding beat of her heart and the next, she knew the answer.

"Yes."

Twelve

By the time the vet left, Cass felt exhausted. Her arm still ached from the booster, and the bandages over the deeper cuts on her arm itched. Chance walked the man out, and only then did she stop to wonder why there'd been no mention of the bill at all. She stroked the colt's neck, hoping her touch would keep him calm. The vet had done what he could, telling her to watch him for further signs of distress and to call if Doc wasn't better in a few hours. They'd have to get him on his feet every hour or so and walk him to help ease the blockage in his intestines.

Colic. One of the worst things that could happen to a horse. The little guy snuffled as he labored to breathe, and her eyes prickled with tears as she listened to him wheeze. She'd considered selling him as a way to get money, but she knew she couldn't, especially not now. Buddy crept into the stall and curled in beside her, his head on her knee. The dog whined softly and stared up at her with big brown eyes as if to say, *I have faith in you. You're my human. You'll make it right.* She ruffled his ears.

"I hope so, Buddy. I hope so."

Chance reappeared moments later, Boots a few steps behind. The older man carried a couple of quilts and a pillow. Chance had mugs of coffee and handed her one. She accepted the cup and stared at its contents. Muddy brown.

Just the right color when cream and coffee achieved the perfect blend.

"One sugar, right?"

She nodded dumbly. The man remembered how she drank her coffee?

"Thought you might as well be comfortable, baby girl." Boots's voice broke her rumination. He spread out one quilt after shooing Buddy away and left the other folded on top with the pillow. "Gonna be a long night." He turned toward Chance, and Cass recognized a look of distrust crossing Boots's face.

"I'll stay up with Cass, Boots. I'll call if we need help."

There was that look again. Cass's attention ping-ponged between the two men. There was definitely defiance and dismissal in Chance's voice, along with a hint of challenge, but Boots didn't rise to the occasion. Instead, he focused on her.

"You need anything at all, baby girl, you just holler. I'll come running."

Cass made a show of straightening the quilt and getting settled on it as the older man shuffled out. She stretched out on her side, the pillow bunched under her head, one hand stroking the colt's neck. An uncomfortable silence descended on the stall, but she wasn't going to be the one to break it. She fidgeted but couldn't get comfortable. After thirty minutes, she gave up.

"We should try to get him on his feet and walk him."

Chance said nothing as he stood and helped her push and pull the colt. Only a yearling, the little guy wasn't close to being full grown, but he was big enough the two of them had trouble. He wobbled on his legs but managed a few tentative steps as Cass led him from the stall. She walked him up and down the center run of the barn so many times she lost count but by the time her legs started to ache, the colt walked a little easier. Once back in the stall, though, he flopped in the straw with a distressed whinny.

Chance had rearranged the blanket and pillow, and now sank down on the quilt before Cass could say anything. He patted the space next to him. She made a face but joined him, realizing too late that he'd raised his arm, and she was now snuggled up against his side. Her nostrils flared at the scent of his cologne, and her stomach did a darn good impression of a bowl of gelatin.

Why did this man tie her up in knots physically and emotionally? What would be so terrible about just letting go, letting him take some of her troubles? Not forever. No, not that. She could never relinquish control forever, but what was the harm in sharing the burden just for a little while? Just long enough to get back on her feet.

"I don't think I'm going back to Chicago." She felt him stiffen.

"Oh?" He said the word carefully.

"I can't leave here. Not yet anyway. I had my neighbor box up or sell all my stuff. It might not be much, but this is home." Something shifted in her heart. Home. This had always been home, and she'd been too blind to realize it.

"That's not true, Cass." She started to bristle, but his hand squeezed her shoulder and she realized he'd relaxed. "This place is a helluva lot. Your dad worked hard to build the Crazy M and to make a home for you. You might not have wanted to be here, but you knew you could always come back."

She nodded, her cheek rubbing against the soft material of his shirt. "I tried to run away. Then I tried to stay away. And then I felt guilty because I hated this place. But I really didn't." She squiggled her nose to chase away the burn of forming tears. "Do you think Daddy understood? Did he know why I wasn't here?"

Chance dropped a kiss on the top of her head. "Did you get to say goodbye?"

Cass inhaled and held her breath to ease the pain in her chest. Exhaling slowly, she shook her head. She had to swallow before she could speak. "Sort of. I was on the phone with him when he passed." She felt Chance wince, and she brushed her palm along his abdomen. "That night at the hotel. In Chicago. I waited too long and got caught by that blizzard. Boots put the phone by Daddy's ear. He...he told me cowgirls don't cry. They just get back on and ride. He used to say that when I was little." She snuggled closer to Chance, seeking his warmth and the gentleness of his embrace. "I guess I've been doing that ever since I got here."

He tilted her head and leaned down to kiss her. His lips, full and firm, danced across her mouth as if seeking permission. She pressed into the kiss, her lips parting in invitation. His hand caressed her side and his fingertips teased the swell of her breast before his palm cupped her fully. Her breath hitched as she sighed.

Cass trailed her hand down those firm, rippled abs of his and found what really interested her. Oh, yeah. He was glad to see her. She stroked him through his jeans and he arched against her hand.

"Damn, girl. I want you."

Not the most romantic of declarations, yet it went straight to her core. She wanted him with a fierceness she'd never experienced. She freed her other arm and fumbled with his buttons.

"Here, let me."

While he dealt with his buttons, fly and boots, she did the same. She kicked off her boots, peeled out of her jeans and T-shirt and was down to her bra and panties when he growled, "No. Mine." She stopped as he took over. He was already naked, but she didn't have time to admire him. His mouth covered hers as he unhooked her bra and slipped its straps off her shoulders.

"You are so beautiful, Cassidy Morgan." He whispered it against her skin as his mouth dipped to find a nipple.

She bowed her back and threaded her fingers through his hair. Oh, the things this man could do with his tongue. She squirmed, pressing her thighs together. One of his hands dipped low, and his strong fingers found her wet and ready. He groaned against her breast, and his erection pressed against her thigh.

Cass wrapped her fingers around his shaft and he groaned again, only this time, he tried to say something. He raised his head to gaze at her, his face flushed and his eyes radiating desire and regret.

He inhaled sharply and finally managed a complete sentence. "I want to be inside you, darlin', but I don't have a condom."

She was so with that program because that's exactly where she wanted him. Until he admitted he wasn't a Boy Scout. "Oh." That one syllable was filled with disappointment. But at the same time, she had to respect him. She stroked his erection and offered a little smile. "We go to Plan B?"

He blinked at her, his confusion showing in his expression. She wiggled loose and kissed her way down his chest. The moment he figured out her intentions, all the air whooshed from his lungs. Gripping him in one hand, she held him still as she wet her lips with her tongue, her eyes glued on his face. He gulped and held his breath. She dipped her head, and her lips glided over him. His hands clutched her head, fingers fighting her ponytail until her hair fell around her shoulders. He held her still for a moment as he throbbed against her palm.

"Easy, baby. I'm already primed."

She raised her head but not before giving him a swirl

with her tongue. "I'll be gentle." She didn't hide the smirk on her face, and after a wink and a cheeky grin, she went back to work.

Chance thought he might die before she finished him off. Cassie had tricks he'd never experienced, and he'd experienced a lot. Sated and lazy, he managed to pull her up to lay next to him, her head just below his shoulder. He hugged her loosely with one arm as her hand alternated between playing with the hair on his chest and places lower.

He was not a man who kept a woman in his bed overnight, but he wanted to spend the night with this woman in his arms—wanted to spend every night with her. He hadn't dated anyone else since he'd first seen her in Chicago; hadn't even looked at other women. He had feelings for her but couldn't define them. The Barrons didn't exactly have a great track record when it came to long-term relationships. Yet this woman touched something deep inside him—a place he wasn't aware of until she came into his life.

He kissed the top of her head and breathed her in. Her hair smelled faintly of sweat and citrus, and his stomach tightened. She nuzzled his skin in a sleepy kiss, and he settled in just to hold her. He'd make sure she was as satisfied as she'd made him when she woke up. For now, she seemed as content as he was.

A few minutes later, the colt stirred but didn't try to get up. Cass awoke instantly but Chance tightened his arms around her. "He's just moving around, darlin'. It's okay. We'll walk him here in a few minutes. First, though, I have my own Plan B to implement."

Her lips curled in a cat-and-cream smile, and her eyes twinkled. He slid down her body until he found a breast. With lips and tongue, he started a slow, sweet assault, gratified when her breath hitched and her legs twitched. He smoothed a hand down her side and cupped the curve of her ass for a gentle squeeze before he pulled her knee over his hip. His fingers dipped lower, finding her sweet spot. Her sharp exhalation ruffled his hair and he smiled, his tongue still flicking over her pebbled nipple. He pushed one finger inside her, and her inner muscles gripped him with wet ferocity. He added a second and she rocked against his hand. He let her set the pace. This time was for her. All her. He wanted her to come saying his name.

Cass panted, and each breath pushed her breast against his tongue. He discovered that his own breathing matched hers, and even as her heart thundered beneath his ear, his heart galloped along. He hardened to the point of pain but didn't care. His fingers caressed and teased, driving her hips to thrust harder and faster. He found her magic button with his thumb and savored her gasp.

"Yes. Yes…oh, yes." She didn't shout it, she whimpered. And that was even sweeter to his ears.

His erection throbbed in time to the clenches her muscles made around his fingers. He rubbed against her firm thigh, the friction making him even harder.

"C'mon, baby. That's my girl. Come for me. Show me how beautiful you are."

"Oh, Chance." His name sighed across her lips and he felt himself tighten. Damned if he wasn't going to come again, with her this time.

"That's it, honey. Yes. C'mon." His hips surged against her, rocking with the same rhythm as hers.

She whimpered, and a soft cry escaped right before she inhaled. A shudder rocked her body, and he exploded as she called his name. "Chance!"

Her fingers dug into his shoulders, and he lifted his head, seeking her lips. He kissed her. Long and hard and deep, his tongue sweeping across hers, his lips branding hers.

"I love you."

The words hung in the dusty air between them. Had he said them out loud? Her body quivered with little aftershocks, and she sighed, her warm breath both tickling and cooling his heated skin. His heart seemed to hesitate between beats as he waited for her reaction.

"Me, too, you."

His heart started again, steady this time, and he breathed. Those three words were enough for now. He cradled her against his side and let her doze. He'd get up and dressed in a few minutes and walk the colt. Until then, he wanted nothing more from life than this woman in his arms.

Now that he'd admitted his feelings aloud, Chance needed this respite from his guilt—and his indecision. He could follow his heart, betray his family and love the woman in his arms. Or he could betray her. The choices sucked, and the devil sitting on his shoulder whispered that he'd resent Cassie for driving a wedge between him and his brothers. He cursed softly even as he tightened his arms around the woman who was becoming his everything.

An hour later, he had the colt up and moving. Cassie watched him, her face pale, and the corners of her mouth drawn down.

"This is all my fault."

Chance continued walking the colt, but he glanced over his shoulder to study her. Her jeans hung low on her hips because she hadn't fastened the top button. The T-shirt she'd pulled on sans bra showed every curve, and he was glad he hadn't fastened his own fly.

"No, it's not. Horses colic, Cassie. I checked the grain bin and the hay. It's all good. No mold. He didn't get sick from eating it. Besides, he's been grazing on grass in the pasture and probably not drinking enough water. You did not do this to him."

She looked so miserable he felt compelled to do something—anything to make her feel better. He'd made love to this woman—*his* woman. And wasn't that a kick in the pants. He hated seeing her so emotionally beaten. As he returned, he paused long enough to gather her into his arms. He kissed her forehead and laid his cheek on the top of her head for a moment. A feeling of rightness settled somewhere in his chest. Despite all the roadblocks, he wanted her—in his bed and in his life.

"I repeat, Cass. This is not your fault. And we'll get him through it. I promise." He planned to promise her so much more, too.

"Don't make promises you can't keep, Chance."

Thirteen

"Shut up, Cord."

Chance's brother was waving a piece of paper in his face. "Have you seen these fliers? Every store in Cowtown has one stuck to the door." He used the local nickname for the area known as Stockyard City.

Chance brushed Cord back with a wave of his hand. "I've seen it. So what?"

"So what? All hell would break out if the old man was here. You better be glad he and Cash flew to Vegas to pull Chase's butt out of the fire over the deal with that showgirl."

He vaguely remembered something about a blackmail scheme and a showgirl at the Barron Crown Casino, and being glad at the time they hadn't dragged him into it. "What do you want me to do about the fliers, Cord? Go door to door and rip them down?"

"I want you to fix this. Before the old man gets back and has a stroke."

"I can't stop her, Cord."

"You can't? Or you won't?"

"Does it matter? Either way, I'm not getting involved."

"You're already involved, Chance. You can't have your cake and eat it, too. Not this time. Do what you always do. Take the bitch—"

Before he knew what happened, Chance had surged from his desk chair and wrapped his fist in his brother's shirtfront. "Don't call her that. Cassidy Morgan is not that kind of woman." Cord grabbed his wrist and squeezed, but Chance didn't loosen his grip.

Cord stared at him, his arched brow speaking volumes.

With studied care, Chance released his brother and leaned back in his chair. Cord retreated to the far side of the desk and tried to look nonchalant as he lounged in one of the armchairs. They stared at each other as the clock ticked off several minutes. Cord finally broke the silence.

"So what are you going to do?"

"Nothing."

"Nothing? What does that mean?"

"Just what it sounds like. Nothing. I'm not going to stop her. I'm not going to help her. I don't think she can pull this thing off. If she does, I'll be surprised, but damn proud of her. It won't matter what we do. She's not giving up." He scrubbed at his forehead with his fingers and willed his headache away. "If the old man had listened to me in the first place, we could have bought her out, and she'd be back in Chicago, safe."

"Safe?"

"Safely out of our hair."

"Yeah. Right. I'm sure that's what you meant. But the old man doesn't work that way, Chance. You know it. I know it. The world knows it. If he finds out about this, it's your ass."

"I'm aware of that, Cord. But…"

"But what?"

"She trusts me."

"Well…crap."

Cass leaned on the stall door and watched as Doc dipped his muzzle in the water trough. She'd just emptied it and re-filled it with fresh. She'd meticulously picked over the hay and grain she put in his manger. Chance had been right. No mold. She rubbed at eyes gritty from lack of sleep. Chance had been right about the colt, too. Doc was fine this morning, seemingly no worse for the wear. She'd have to muck out his stall soon, but this was one time she wouldn't complain. Not one bit.

Boots joined her. His appraising eye roamed over the horse and the stall. "He's gonna be fine, baby girl." He nudged her with his shoulder. "And I have news about your flyers. We'll have some help with the herd."

She glanced at him as he continued.

"The agriculture teacher over from the high school called. He's got some FFA boys comin' to round up the herd and get 'em gathered here in the big pasture today. Some of 'em are gonna make the ride with us, too. They get extra credit."

Future Farmers of America. Now that was a group she hadn't thought about in years. She'd been the FFA queen one year and sold a bunch of World's Finest Chocolate to help with votes. "What goes around comes around," she chuckled.

"We need to get those cows started tomorrow, Cassie. Big sale is on Friday mornin'. The cattle need to be penned and ready in the stockyards by Thursday night."

She rubbed her eyes again and rolled her head, listening to the familiar snap and crackle as vertebrae ground together at the top of her spine. "I got all the permits for Canadian County. And the commissioner from Oklahoma County says he'll have a set ready today."

"Nadine's offered to feed everyone. She's shuttin' down the Four Corners and is gonna drive her RV. She'll set up camp for us and have food ready for the crew mornin' and night."

"But…she can't close the diner. She'll lose too much money, Uncle Boots."

He patted her shoulder, his grin adding more crinkles to his weatherworn cheeks. "Honey, she wouldn't miss this for the world. She closes a week for vacation ever year anyway, so this is her vacation."

Cass rubbed her chest to ease the tightness forming there. "This is going to work, Uncle Boots."

"Yup."

Boots could be a man of few words. "I guess I'd better go pick up those permits, huh?"

"Yup." He dug in his pocket and handed over the keys to the truck.

Cass perched on the tailgate of Boots's truck and tried not to laugh. She really did. But the sight of the group of high school kids flapping their arms and waving their hats as they tried to funnel the herd through the gate while on foot had her doubled over. She lightly punched Boots's arm as he leaned next to her.

"That's just mean."

"Yup."

The ag teacher laughed along with her. "They need to taste a little vinegar. Ranching is hard. The sooner they learn that, the better. This life isn't a glorified Western movie."

"Boy, isn't that the truth!"

"Still, I'm always reminded of that speech John Wayne makes in the movie *McClintock*. The one where he's talking to his daughter about how he didn't plan to leave her the whole ranch, just a little start-up place. There's a whole lot of growing a person has to do to become a rancher."

Cass stared at the teacher, struck dumb by the revelation. She watched the kids work, sober now in her reflections. In many ways, her dad had given her that same speech—but in his actions, not his words. She ran off to the world and forgot the lessons she'd learned here in this place. She'd forgotten what home felt like. And now she remembered. Thanks to Boots. And Chance.

Her heart burned with fierce pride for the first time in ten years. She turned her head slightly to look at Boots, and a small smile hovered at the corner of her mouth. Squeezing the old man's arm, she leaned in and planted an impulsive kiss on his cheek.

"What was that for?"

"For helping me realize that I'm home." She laughed as a boy tripped and face-planted in the pasture. A girl helped him up, and the two of them jogged after a steer refusing to go through the gate. "God help me with that bunch, but by golly, we're going to get this herd to market!"

Chance's absence kept this from being perfect. She knew he was busy. Lawyers with their own law firms were. Her feelings for him were still new enough she hadn't figured out the rules. Cass did know that what she felt for Chance was all tied up with her feelings of coming home.

Early the next morning, Nadine's RV idled in the front yard. She'd arrived at the crack of dawn and already had coffee and doughnuts ready for folks as they arrived. Horse trailers and pickups littered the yard and people milled about. Saddled horses stood tied, swishing desultory tails at the occasional fly, heads down as they dozed in the early-morning light.

Cass hadn't slept much. Keyed up, nervous and scared she'd fail, she'd paced the floor of her bedroom in between bouts of tossing and turning. She wished Chance was there—even if Boots would have a conniption over Chance sharing her bed. She wanted the comfort of his arms. He would have kissed her, told her she was doing the right thing and that everything would be all right.

He's busy, she told herself, but part of her resented the fact he wasn't there. He'd said the words, told her he loved her, but everything was still new enough, she didn't know whether to believe or not. Especially when it seemed that if she needed him, he couldn't, or wouldn't, make time.

She had four days to go just over twenty miles with five hundred head of prime grass-fed beef. At current market rates, they were selling for almost a hundred and fifty dollars for a hundredweight. Even if they brought less, she'd make enough to pay off the mortgage and her dad's medical bills.

Nadine pressed a steaming cup of coffee in her hand. "I made it good and strong this morning, honey. Y'all are gonna need a kick in the britches today."

Without thinking, Cass took a sip and sputtered. She managed to swallow the hot, black liquid without spitting, but it took supreme effort on her part.

"Cream and sugar is over there, hon." Nadine patted her on the back in an effort to ease her coughing spasm.

"Thanks." The word came out choked but at least she could still talk. Movement down at the gate caught her eye. The big Ford pickup maneuvered through the congestion and inched up the drive. Chance. Had he come to help after all? She waited until he parked before walking over. She arrived just as he stepped out.

He wore boots, but he sure wasn't dressed for cowboy work. Dress slacks and a starched button-down shirt made him look more like a male model than ever. Or a lawyer. But what she wanted right then was a cowboy. She schooled her expression before greeting him.

"Hi, cowboy, fancy meeting you here." She kept her voice light and teasing despite the disappointment churning inside her. That whole fantasy of the two of them riding off into the sunset was just that. A fantasy. For now at least.

"I have court today, Cass. I'm sorry. I couldn't get the docket changed." He didn't step away from the shelter provided by the open door and the bulk of the truck cab. Truth be told, she was glad for the privacy.

She lifted one shoulder in a lopsided shrug. "Hey, work happens. Thanks for getting up so early to come see us off."

He gazed around and seemed surprised by the hustle and bustle and the number of people. "Looks like you have a lot of help."

"Yeah. We even have places to camp out along the way. Once the word got out about what I'm doing, all sorts of people stepped up." She inhaled, feeling very pleased with herself. "This will work, Chance. I'm going to get the herd to the stockyards and get them sold. Then I can pay off Daddy's debts."

"What will you do then?"

His voice sounded peculiar, and she cut her eyes in his direction. He looked odd, the expression on his face unreadable. She tilted her head and turned to face him. "I'm staying here. Daddy's dying gift to me was that colt down in the barn. I'm not a rancher. I don't know squat about cows, but horses? Horses I know. I'll use any money left over from the sale to get a couple of mares and when Doc is old enough, I'll breed him. And I'll train horses. I may have been out of the game for ten years, but I went out on top. I was the national champion cowgirl."

Cass watched his Adam's apple bob as he swallowed then lifted her gaze to his eyes. He looked almost…haunted for a moment, and she wondered why. He blinked, and his expression changed. What lurked behind the smile he now wore?

"So you *are* a cowgirl at heart."

His teasing sounded forced to her ears, but she returned his smile with a hesitant one of her own. "Guess I always was. Just took coming home—and a certain cowboy—to make me remember that."

She glanced to the eastern horizon where the top curve of the morning sun had cleared the tree line. "Time to get this party started." She rocked up on her toes and brushed her lips across his, her palm braced against his chest for balance. "Thanks for coming to see me off."

There was nothing forced about his smile as his arm circled her waist and hugged her a bit closer. "I wouldn't have missed this for the world." He kissed her back, deeply, his lips nibbling hers as his tongue eased into her mouth to tease her.

A bit breathless when he released her, she rocked back on her heels and figured she looked either bemused or just plain stupid because wow. That man could kiss her right out of her boots.

Chance laughed, obviously pleased by her reaction. He placed his hands on her shoulders and turned her around. "Head 'em up, cowgirl."

In less time than she anticipated, her drovers had the herd lined up and ready to move out of the pasture and onto the road. Boots had cut part of the fence to install a temporary gate, and one of the neighbors would restring the barbed wire once the herd was well on its way. The old man sat on his horse at the opening, waiting to lead the herd. Cass held Red's reins, and was about to mount and give the order to move out when a car flew up the road scattering a dust cloud in its wake. The vehicle, with no apparent attempt to brake, careened into her drive.

"What the hell?" She dropped the reins and marched toward the car, which had stopped. She noticed that Boots was riding up at a gallop.

The white, four-door sedan looked like an unmarked police car. The vehicle even had a spotlight mounted above the driver's-side mirror. She stopped a few feet away, fists planted on her hips as she waited for the driver to emerge. She expected to see a uniform. She got a nondescript man wearing cheap khaki pants and a blue short-sleeved shirt that looked in desperate need of an iron.

"I'm lookin' for Cassidy Morgan!" The man bawled out her name at the top of his lungs. All eyes turned in her direction.

"That would be me. Who are you?"

He walked up and waved an envelope under her nose. "Here."

She refused to take it. "What's that?"

He stuffed it down the front of her shirt. "You've been served."

"What?" Cass dug the envelope out of her shirt and tore it open. She read the heading, "In the District Court of the County of Oklahoma, State of Oklahoma." Her eyes skipped down, caught her name and the name of the bank, followed by the words "wholly owned subsidiary of Barron Enterprises" before focusing on the first paragraph. "What the hell?"

"That, Miss Morgan, is a foreclosure notice. Everything on this ranch now belongs to Barron Enterprises by way of Stockmen's Bank and Trust."

She stared at him, her mouth gaping. She shook her head and bit back the curses she wanted to spew in his direction. Instead, she read the notice. "This is bull. It says there's a hearing set for next Monday. I have until then to present collateral assets or to pay off the loan." She thought. The legal terms were jumbled in her head and then she remembered. Chance! He was an attorney.

Before she could call him over, the process server called out. "Mr. Barron! I didn't see you, sir."

Mr. *Barron*? There was a Barron on her property? She whipped her head around to see who the man was talking to.

One look at Chance's face and she knew.

Oh, God. His last name—the one she'd assumed was Chancellor—was Barron. Her heart shriveled in her chest, and she couldn't breathe. Only sheer stubbornness kept her standing.

"Chance?" His name tumbled out before she could stop herself. "Please...tell me this isn't happening." But she knew. Her head knew even as her heart tried to hide from the pain. His expression said it all. Her stomach knotted, and she swallowed hard to keep the bile rising in her throat at bay.

"Cassidy." Her name, a whisper from his lying lips, sighed on the morning breeze.

God, but she was stupid. Chance. Chancellor Barron. Even in Chicago she'd heard the names of all the Barron brothers. How had she not recognized him? Would it have mattered? She'd wanted him that night in his condo, and again in the barn and every other time they'd been together. She'd wanted him, and she'd allowed herself to fall in love with him.

"Please, Cassie…" Her name dripped off his tongue like honey, and he tried to look sincere and repentant but she didn't buy his act for a minute.

"Please Cassie what? Please Cassie let me steal your home? Or please Cassie let me screw you one more time?" She wadded up the paper in her hand and threw it at his face. She scored a direct hit, but he didn't even flinch. "Get the hell off my land."

He grabbed her forearm and squeezed just hard enough she couldn't jerk away. Cass stared down at his hand—tanned, strong and belonging to a liar. She was such a fool. One night of mind-blowing sex with him and he'd gotten under her skin—and into her heart. And that one night had turned into so much more. She'd started dreaming—of him, of life with him here on the ranch. She loved him. Or did. Before he betrayed her. Her face flushed with anger as she raised her gaze to collide with his.

"Please, Cassie. Let me explain."

"Move it or lose it, Mr. *Barron*."

If anything, his grip tightened, and for a moment, she got lost in his amber eyes. Then she remembered he was nothing more than a predator. A snake. A…she didn't want to malign innocent members of the animal kingdom so she called a spade a spade. "Let me go, you bastard. You lied to me. And you cheated me. I…I thought you cared. About me. About the ranch. God, how could I have been so damned wrong about you? About…us."

Her voice cracked, and his grip loosened slightly. She jerked her arm out of his grasp, no longer caring that her voice quivered. "Get away from me, Chance. I hate you. I hate everything you stand for. I'll put a certified check for the full amount of the loan on your desk by five o'clock Friday afternoon. I have a herd of cattle to get to market so get the hell out of my way."

She turned on her heel and marched over to Boots where he stood holding the reins of her horse. She snatched them and stood glaring at him.

"You knew." Oh yeah, he knew all right. "Why didn't you tell me?"

"I was waitin' for him t'do the right thing."

"Seriously? He's a friggin' Barron, Uncle Boots." She dashed at her eyes with the back of her hand. She'd be damned if she shed tears over Chance Barron. Not now. Not ever. "He wouldn't know the right thing if it walked up and bit him on the ass."

Cass swung up on the big sorrel, and settled into the saddle. Boots touched her knee.

"I'm sorry, baby girl."

She closed her eyes and fought for control as Boots mounted his horse. The man never did anything without a good reason. Someday, maybe she wouldn't hurt so much, and she could talk about it. Not now. Now she had a herd to deliver.

Buddy barked and quivered with excitement. She glanced at her handful of drovers and though she tried not to, she had to glance at Chance. He hadn't moved and his face looked as if it had been carved from granite for all the emotion he showed. Fine. She didn't need him. Twenty miles from the ranch to the stockyards with five hundred head of cattle. If she pulled this off, it would be a miracle. She had to be as crazy as a grasshopper sunbathing on a red ant pile.

Fourteen

Chance recognized the stubborn jut of her chin and had to admire her despite the fact he pretty much hated himself as much as she claimed to hate him. She'd mounted her horse with controlled elegance and didn't take out her obvious anger on the sorrel. The grim set of her mouth didn't diminish her beauty. She wheeled Red around to face the people who'd gathered.

Despite angry looks from other bystanders, he stepped back to the front fender of his truck to watch. This moment belonged to Cassie. He might have destroyed any hope for a relationship but he still cared, still loved her. Cyrus Barron would never be able to take his feelings for her away. Chance had wanted her to have this moment of glory, even if it turned into a last hurrah. He would track down who tried to rob it from her.

"This is it," she called. "Cyrus Barron has decided I'm public enemy number one. Some of you might not want to get on his bad side. I'll understand if you drop out. No hard feelings. But I'm mad as hell, and I'm going to prove to that old bastard that he can knock me down, but I won't stay in the dirt."

She straightened her shoulders and stood in her stirrups. "My daddy didn't know what giving up meant. I'm not about to let him down now. I have four days to get these cows to the stockyards and by God, I'm gonna get 'em there come hell, high water or the damned Barron family!"

Cheers answered her, and he couldn't suppress the feeling of pride welling inside him. And apprehension. If he knew his father, she would have both hell and high water to deal with.

She laughed, but it sounded mirthless in the fading echoes of the shouts of the drovers. "I've always wanted to say this! Head 'em up! Move 'em out!"

Chance waited until the last steer and the drag riders disappeared up the road. Two men patched the fence, and Nadine rolled up the awning on her RV. She walked over and leaned on the truck fender next to him.

"You should'a told her." The woman gazed eastward where a red haze still hung in the still air.

"Probably." He watched the same dust cloud.

"You care about her."

"Probably." Hell, yeah, he cared. He loved her. But he couldn't admit it. Not out loud. He'd told Cass and look what happened. He hung his head and refused to meet Nadine's knowing gaze.

"So what are you going to do about it?"

"Damned if I know, Nadine."

She chuckled and smacked his arm. He resisted the urge to rub the spot. For a woman her age, she still carried quite a punch. "Then it's high time you figured it out, Chancellor Barron. She's worth fightin' for."

Nadine walked away before he could reply. He watched her climb into the big RV then maneuver it over the rutted yard. Once she had the nose of the vehicle pointed in the right direction, she tooted the horn and waved at him as she headed off.

His phone vibrated on his hip. Tempted to ignore it, he checked the caller ID anyway. His brother Cash.

"What?"

"Did I catch you in the middle of something?"

"What do you want, Cash?"

"If I'd known you were going to be at the Morgan place this morning, I could have saved money on the process server."

"You're the one who sent him out here?"

"Well…yeah. The old man said you were busy. Since you hadn't done it yet, he had the papers filed yesterday and wanted them served first thing."

"Yeah, I just bet he did."

"Whoa, Chance. You sound pissed."

"I am."

"Hey, I was just following the old man's orders. You want to tell me what's going on?"

"No. But fair warning, Cash. You ever again go behind my back to serve papers without my go-ahead, you'll regret it." He stabbed the end button on his phone and tossed it onto the center console of the truck. Within seconds, it danced across the leather. He ignored it. Gazing around, he realized his family might have more money than many small countries, but Cass Morgan was far richer.

After three days on the trail, Cass would give just about anything she owned for a hot shower lasting longer than five minutes. It was hard to do much more than sluice off the surface dust in the tepid water and confined space of the tiny shower in Nadine's RV. Her hair hung dull and limp when she removed the ponytail holder.

A new set of volunteers had arrived each day to help as drovers and outriders. The nightly camps had a holiday air as folks visited and relaxed once the herd was settled for the night. She wished she could unwind and enjoy their camaraderie. But she couldn't. Not until the herd was delivered, sold, and she had the check in her hand.

The RV was parked on the expansive lot of a suburban

acreage. A catering truck from a local BBQ restaurant was on site with a smoker. The scent of roasting beef wafted in the open window. With a grimace at how nasty her hair felt as she combed it with her fingers, she smoothed it back and refastened it into a ponytail. Navigating down the narrow aisle, Cassie smiled at the cowboy chic decor and squeezed past the older woman puttering at the stove. The motorhome was pure Nadine.

Cass pushed the screen door open, stepped out and ran smack dab into a very masculine body.

Chance's hands steadied her until she regained her balance. She scowled at him. "What the hell are you doing here?"

"We need to talk, Cass."

"No, we don't."

"Yes, we do. I had to take care of some things or I would have been here sooner."

She wanted to thump his chest with her fist. Or slap him. "Go away, Chance. I don't need or want you."

"Look, you have every reason to be upset—"

"Ya think? You lied to me."

"No. Not technically speaking."

"What? You lied about your name."

"No, I didn't."

"Yes, you did."

"No. When I first introduced myself, I said my name was Chancellor. *You* jumped the gun and assumed it was my last name."

"Well, you weren't in any hurry to correct that assumption, were you?" He flushed at that, and she pressed home her point. "And you never made any attempt to set me straight."

"Technically, you never asked for clarification, Cass."

She blinked at him, opened her mouth and closed it, at a loss for words for a moment. "Technically? Freaking lawyer. I shouldn't have had to. You led me on, Chance. You let me believe you were somebody else. Somebody I could—"

She snapped her jaw shut. She would never admit to this man how much she had trusted him, how much he had hurt her. She let him hurt her by caring about him. By…no. She refused to acknowledge that she loved him.

Chance hung his head and looked penitent. She didn't believe the pose for a New York minute. "Cass, please? I can explain. Things are different now."

"Different? You mean you didn't actually file a foreclosure action for your father? That you don't mean to steal the ranch from me? Throw me out on my butt? Jeez, Chance. You can't even admit that I was nothing but a piece of ass to you." Her eyelids prickled, but she'd be damned if she'd cry.

"Don't be mad, Cass. Just listen to me."

"Mad? I don't get mad, Chance Barron. I get even."

She pushed past him with a growl, ignoring his outstretched hand, and stomped over to the campfire where Boots and the volunteer wranglers sat. Only Boots had the guts to look at her. She stamped her foot, her face flaming from anger. "Ooh. That man makes me crazy, Uncle Boots."

He patted the folding chair next to him. "Take a load off, honey. I get the feeling that situation goes both ways. You make Chance Barron a little crazy, too."

Cass dropped into the chair and stretched her legs out. Inhaling slow, measured breaths, she glanced at the old man from the corner of her eye and caught a flicker of movement. Chance actually had the nerve to walk closer. She reached for the shotgun lying across the ice chest beside her chair and placed it across her thighs. Not that she'd actually use it. Chance took another step, and she checked the breach to see if the gun was loaded.

Boots chuckled as Chance retreated without turning his back. "Discretion is the better part of valor, I guess."

She watched Chance retreat. "What the hell does that mean, Uncle Boots?"

"It means you've got the man tied up in knots, honey. He wants you. Wants you enough to stand up to his daddy to get you." Boots inclined his head toward the picket line, the rope stretched between two trees where the trail horses were loosely tied for the night. He watched her face to make sure she paid attention. A television reporter and camera-man interviewed one of her volunteers, who was brushing his horse, for the evening news. "Who do you think alerted the media? Why do you think we suddenly got all this attention and more riders?"

"Ha! I don't believe that at all."

Nadine stuck her head out of the RV. "Well, you better believe it, Cassie. They got a call from Chance's office, least ways that's what the producer feller told me. Your story is all over the news. Here and nationally. All the networks picked it up. Considering Cyrus Barron owns the news-papers around here and a bunch of TV and radio stations, just how else do you think the national folks tumbled to this little shindig?"

Cass leaned back in the chair and swiveled her head just far enough to keep track of Chance. He'd walked back to his pickup truck and leaned against the front fender talking to another man just as tall, dark and handsome. Had to be one of his brothers but for her life, she didn't know which one.

"Why would he do that?"

"He loves you."

"He's in love."

Boots said it first, but Nadine's assertion echoed a half beat later. No. Nonononono no! This wasn't happening. Chance Barron didn't love her. He couldn't. He just wanted the ranch so his father could erase all memory of Ben Mor-gan from the face of the earth.

Cass had finally finagled the full story out of Boots—

how Cyrus had pursued her mom but she'd married her dad instead. She couldn't fathom why a man as rich and powerful as the senior Barron carried such a long-standing grudge. Three hard days in the saddle had rubbed the furious off her temper, though she remained miffed at the old man for not telling her Chance's real identity.

Boots's revelation over Chance's feelings left her own unsteady. When she realized her hand was still curled around the shotgun, she carefully placed it back on the ice chest.

"No. I can't deal with this. Not now. I have five hundred head of cattle to get to market. And one more day to get it done."

"We've made good distance, Cass. We only have about five miles to go."

She closed her eyes and laid her head back against the chair. "It might as well be a thousand, Uncle Boots. We hit the county line tomorrow. You know Cyrus Barron will have every deputy in Oklahoma County lined up to keep us out. Even though I managed to get the permits from Oklahoma County, I don't believe for a second they'll be worth the paper they're printed on. Even if the sheriff and his deputies don't stop us, there'll be the whole Oklahoma City Police Department waiting at the city limits. The Barrons always get their way."

"You forget, hon. The media will be there, too. Sheriff Wallace is up for reelection. You're a huge story." Hands on her ample hips, Nadine climbed down the steps and stopped right in front of Cass. "You're the underdog. The pretty little girl takin' on the big bads with a ragtag group of volunteers. From the information the national outlets are reporting? You can bet someone on the inside spilled the beans. Mr. Chance Barron, in fact."

Cass shook her head, unable to believe Chance would stand up to his father. "What's in it for him?"

Nadine chuckled. "A pretty little blonde who hog-tied his heart."

"No. There's something more. He doesn't love me. If he loved me, he wouldn't have lied. And he damn sure wouldn't have betrayed me like he did."

The rumbling bass thrum of a diesel engine caught her attention. Chance and the man he was with had climbed into the pickup. She watched as Chance carefully backed the truck onto the road and headed east. The bright lights of Oklahoma City shone like jewels scattered on a pair of faded jeans.

Yeah. He loved her all right. He'd tucked his tail between his legs and slunk off like the dirty dog he was.

Buddy whined, almost as if he'd read her thoughts. She dropped her hand to his head and scratched his ears. "No offense, Buddy," she murmured.

The dog growled softly in reply but dropped his chin to the toe of her boot and settled in for a nap. He'd worked hard, and she was going to buy him the biggest steak Cattlemen's Cafe had on the menu once the herd was delivered to the stockyards. She had the cash in her pocket to buy that steak—and one for Boots and Nadine, too.

Chance ignored his brother as he gunned the big diesel engine of his Ford F250. "I know what I'm doing, Cord."

"No, Chance. You don't. The old man is already stroking out from this mess. How the hell did the national media get this story?"

"I told them."

"You what? Damn, little brother. Do you have a death wish? The old man is going to cut you off at the knees."

"He can try, Cord." He moistened dry lips with a tongue resembling sandpaper and loosened his white-knuckled grip on the steering wheel. "Look, we all know he's being a jerk about this. And he can't get his hands on the ranch anyway."

"Oh? You're that sure she's going to get those cows to the stockyards and sold?"

"Doesn't matter if she does or not. I paid off the mortgage and put the deed solely in her name."

"Oh, hell, son. Tell me that ain't so. The old man will shoot you dead right where you stand." Cord scrubbed fingers through his hair. "Does she know?"

"Not a chance. She'd fight me all the way, Cord. Besides, this is something she has to do on her own. She needs to find out what's important. That what's *here* is important." *That I'm important to her.*

"Do you truly believe she'll be so grateful she throws herself into your arms, kisses you all over and falls in love?"

Chance squirmed in his seat remembering Cassie's kisses. "She's already in love with me, Cord. She just hasn't admitted it yet."

"Dammit, Chance. Are you really going to throw away everything for that girl?"

He didn't hesitate a moment. "Yeah. I am."

Fifteen

Her wristwatch read five minutes after five. Cass sipped the cup of coffee Nadine handed her and watched the sky in the east lighten from cobalt to lapis. Wisps of cloud looked like watercolor brush strokes in shades of sangria and salmon.

"Red sky at morning, sailors take warning." Cass recited the old weather adage.

A voice rumbled behind her. "Well, it's a good thing we aren't on the water, then."

She chuckled as the man stepped up beside her. "G'morning, Uncle Boots."

Nadine handed him a cup, and Cass noticed how their fingers lingered against each other. She'd seen this coming, and it lightened her heart. Nadine and Boots made a good match. Maybe she should just turn over the ranch to the Barrons. Boots and Buddy could move in with Nadine. Cass could choose any city in the country and pick up the pieces of her life.

Not far away, a horse whickered, answered by the lowing moo of one of the cows. She inhaled. The aroma of the coffee in her mug mingled with the hot, acrid smell of dust. Leather, trampled grass and the dry sweet scent of Bermuda hay all hit her nose. And it smelled like home. No. She couldn't give up the ranch. Not now. Not after all the battles she'd fought.

The camp stirred around her. Quiet voices as people finished quick breakfasts were punctuated by the stamp of horses' hooves as they were saddled, the creak of leather and the jangle of bridle bits as riders mounted. An occasional whinny as horses and humans worked to gather the herd added to the music of Buddy's happy barks.

Cass swallowed the last bit of liquid in her cup. "I'll saddle our horses, Uncle Boots. You finish your coffee."

The first vivid scarlet of the sun's curve poked above the horizon. Cass looked at the knot of riders awaiting her signal. This was it. About six miles to the end of her rainbow. She needed a big pot of gold when she reached it. Her throat closed, and she couldn't breathe for a long moment.

Boots nudged his horse up beside hers. "What's up, baby girl?"

Her smile wavered. "Just a memory." At his arched brow and curious head tilt, she continued. "Do you remember the spring Momma died?" He nodded, and she swallowed around the lump. "Lot of storms that year. There was a double rainbow after one of them and Daddy loaded me up in the truck to go chase the end of it. We drove all over three counties, me pointing and shouting out the way. I swear that thing stayed in the sky for a couple of hours. I was so disappointed when it faded away. Daddy held my hand on the way home, even when he had to shift gears. When we got out, he told me that Momma gave me that rainbow— to show me that chasing my dreams was never a waste of time. And to remind me that she'd always watch over us."

Boots cleared his throat then coughed softly. "For such a hard man, Ben was just an old softy when it came to you and your momma, baby girl."

She inhaled and exhaled, her chest rising and falling, but the constriction only lessened slightly. "Daddy's watchin' over me now, Uncle Boots. And I want him to be proud of me." Cass rose in her stirrups and addressed the riders. "Head 'em up, folks. Time to move 'em out."

Buddy barked and raced to the back of the herd. The others reined their horses into position and remained quiet while the drag riders pushed the herd forward. Amid moos and bleats, the cattle milled around then moved forward. Outriders funneled them through the gate of the field where they'd camped. Boots led the way, setting the pace. With fences on either side of the section line road, it was more a matter of keeping the herd moving. They wanted to stop and graze in the right-of-way.

This was their fourth day on the drive, and folks had settled into the rhythm. The occasional whoop and slap of work-gloved hands on leather chaps punctuated the still summer air. Four thousand hooves kicked up a lot of Oklahoma red dirt. Cass wondered how far off the dust cloud could be seen. In less than a mile, they'd hit the Oklahoma County line. The front of the herd was already on paved road, but she seriously doubted she could sneak past the border.

A helicopter buzzed overhead. A few of her volunteers looked up to track its movement. A couple of them waved. National news reporters or local? She shook her head, still surprised by the coverage. She might fail miserably but at least she'd go out in a blaze of glory. She thought of the Bon Jovi song and chuckled.

"Oh, yeah. Cyrus Barron definitely wants me dead or alive. Preferably dead, I'm sure."

Cord led two horses out of the trailer and handed the lead rope of one to Chance. "I can't believe all the legal hoops you've jumped through. Getting recused from the suit and then you got Judge Reynolds to sign the order that'll really put a twist in the Old Man's shorts."

"You don't have to come, Cord. I'm not twisting your arm."

His brother laughed. "No, you aren't. I'm doing it because it'll piss off the old man. Plus, I want to see if this gal is good enough for you."

Chance smoothed the blanket across his horse's withers, grabbed his saddle and tossed it up. He loosely cinched the girth then slipped the halter down as he bridled the animal. "The question is whether or not I'm good enough for her. I screwed this one up royally."

Cord clapped him on the shoulder. "I still can't believe you got Judge Reynolds to sign that order."

He shrugged. "I caught him in the bar at the club. Heidi will file it as soon as the court clerk's office opens, and then she'll deliver a copy to the sheriff's office." He glanced at the expensive watch on his wrist. "I just hope Cass got a late start this morning. She's been driving those cattle from can see to can't see."

Cord chuckled. "You've been reading Louis L'Amour again." He glanced toward the west. A few stars still sparkled faintly against an indigo backdrop. Behind them to the east, the sun was banked by clouds and fiery red rays grabbed at the dark sky. "Red skies, Chance. I hope the weather holds. Getting caught out in a thunderstorm will be a very bad thing."

They tied their horses to the trailer, and Cord grabbed a stainless-steel thermos. He poured coffee into travel mugs and handed one to Chance. "This girl is riding you hard. I'm not sure that's a good thing."

Chance stared off toward the horizon. "She makes me want to be a better man than I am, Cord."

"How's that working for you?"

"Hurts like hell, but I'm going to prove myself to her. I'm going to be that man, come hell or high water."

* * *

Cass put her heels to the big sorrel, and the horse trotted up to join the dun Boots rode. Red whickered, and Lucky answered back. The horses didn't care what was up ahead. She couldn't see over the low rise in front of them, but she knew what waited on the other side. County Line Road. The helicopter still droned overhead, and she could see media trucks set up for remote telecasts. So far she'd declined comment but didn't stop any of her volunteer riders from answering reporters' questions. She rolled her neck. At the snap, crackle and pop, Boots turned to watch her.

"Problem with your neck?"

Her laugh sounded as dry as the red dust coating the weeds lining the road. "Naw. Just stress."

They rode in relative silence but for the thud of hooves, Buddy's excited bark and a few indignant moos. Her horse tossed his head and pulled against the reins. Cass realized she had a death grip on them and loosened her fingers. Red stretched his nose out and shook his head again, which jangled the rings on the bit in his mouth.

"It'll be okay, honey."

"I'm glad you think so, Uncle Boots. Me? I figure I'm on my way to jail as soon as we top that rise."

Before he could reply, two horsemen appeared silhouetted for a moment before they cantered up the road. Her mouth straightened into a grim slash. "Is that Chance? What the hell is he doing here?"

"Don't go jumpin' to conclusions, Cassidy. Let the man talk before you bite his head off."

"And who's with him? Is he wearing a uniform? Is that a deputy?"

"I never knew a deputy to wear a shirt like that, hon."

She shaded her eyes. Chance wore a faded chambray shirt, but the man riding with him wore a bright red plaid with fancy stitching, fringe and pearl buttons. "Okay. That's the worst Western shirt I've ever seen."

"I heard that," the other man called.

The men reined in and waited. When Cass and Boots came even with them, they turned their horses and fell in, Chance riding knee-to-knee on her right and the other man beside him.

"My brother Cord. Cord, Boots Thomas and Cassidy Morgan."

Cord tipped the brim of his hat and pretended to pout. "I dressed up special for this rodeo. I can't believe you're dissin' my shirt."

She had to bite her lip. Cord definitely got all the charm in the family. Working her mouth to keep from grinning, she cast an arch look in their direction. "So why are you here?"

"I have a signed injunction, Cass."

"You what?" She twisted in her saddle and nailed his arm with a fist. "Of all the low-down, cowardly, despicable, low-life..." She sputtered and spit, so angry she couldn't even talk. Without warning, Chance grabbed her, hauled her out of her saddle and settled her across his thighs. His arms pinned hers to her sides but she struggled anyway.

"Dammit, hold still, Cass."

"Let. Me. Guh-uh-uh." His lips sealed on hers, cutting off her last word. She fought him, but as his mouth pressed against hers and his tongue teased her lips open, her struggles lessened, and she relaxed—if pressing against him as her tongue entwined with his could be called relaxing.

With a ragged gasp, he broke the kiss. "Please listen, Cass. The injunction is against the sheriff and the city police. Judge Reynolds signed it so you can continue to drive the herd to Stockyard City."

If someone were to ask later, she'd vow that was not a sob bubbling in her throat. When his arms loosened enough that she could move, she bunched his shirt into her fists and stared at him nose to nose. "Swear you mean that. Swear I'm going to get the herd to the stockyards today so they can go in the sale tomorrow."

"On my honor, Cass. I know my word means nothing to you, but give me a chance to prove myself. That's why Cord and I are here." He kissed her again. "Give me a chance to be the right man for you. To prove how much I love you."

"Oh, hi, Cass. I'm Cord. Chance's older, saner brother. Nice to meet you."

She laughed, unable to stop the swing of emotions from anger to giddy relief with a pit stop at *Ohmygoshhereally-lovesme!* She glanced over at Cord but returned her gaze to stare at Chance, her head slowly shaking from side to side. "Hi, Cord. Nice to meet you. I think." Then she thumped her fist against Chance's chest. "Put me back on my horse, buster. We have a herd to deliver."

"Yes, ma'am!"

A moment later, Chance's strong arms slid from around her, and she was back in her saddle. Behind her, cheers rose in sharp crescendo to the soothing lows from the herd. Did she have a chance to make her dad proud? She didn't dare hope. Not until she'd closed the gate on the last pen at the stockyards. Chance reached over and took her hand, gave it a little squeeze and winked. Her heart danced a two-step in her chest. Then they topped the rise, and her heart stopped. The road was blocked by black sheriff cruisers, the emergency lights on top blazing red and blue.

Sixteen

"Stop right there!" The voice echoed through the bull-horn.

"Keep riding."

She didn't need Chance's urging. "Let's get this over with." She touched her spurs to Red's sides, and the big horse surged to a canter. Chance's horse stayed right beside her. The next thing she knew, Cord had galloped up on her other side. "Gee, we're one horseman short of the Apocalypse." She couldn't resist the quip.

Cord blew out a snort of laughter. "We'll just have to try harder."

She glanced to her left and studied Chance's brother for a long moment. Of similar build, with the same dark hair and brown eyes, they shared some amazing genetics. He rode with a reckless ease even though his expression looked grim and determined. She was suddenly glad these two men rode at her side.

Peeking at Chance, she noticed he was scanning the crowd gathered in the intersection behind the barricade of sheriff's office vehicles. His face lit up, and she followed his gaze to find a petite brunette waving madly. Jealousy twisted in her stomach.

"There's Heidi." Chance stood up in his stirrups to see better. The woman waved again and held up a manila folder.

"She got the filing done. We're good to go. I know it's not your style, Cass, but let me do the talking this time?"

The corner of her mouth quirked in a little grin. He hadn't made that an order but a request. He was learning. "Who's Heidi?" She wanted to bite off her tongue as the question slipped off its tip.

"My paralegal. She filed the injunction and delivered copies first thing this morning."

The constriction in her chest lessened. His paralegal. Just his paralegal. Nobody special. Well, she amended, nobody special to his heart. "Tell her thanks?"

"You can tell her yourself when I introduce you. In the meantime..." He paused and blew out a breath. "I've probably been presumptuous but I'm on file with the court as your attorney. Let me deal with the deputies. Okay?"

"Okay."

Chance rode past Heidi, grabbed the envelope but didn't dismount when they stopped in front of the roadblock. He delivered the signed, if slightly crumpled, order to the deputy with the bullhorn. Words were exchanged, followed by radio transmissions between the deputies and the sheriff's office. Cass sat stiffly, pressing her lips together.

"Easy, Cass. Chance knows what he's doing."

She cut her eyes to Cord. "I sure hope so."

His knee bumped hers as his bay sidled closer to her horse. "You did something to him, Cass. Something good. Don't let pride mess this up for either of you."

She rolled her eyes. "That's easy for you to say."

Chance reined his horse around and rejoined them. "It's done. They're moving their cars. We'll still need to deal with OCPD when we hit the city limits. The good news is, Bethany PD is shutting down traffic and giving us an escort through town. That'll help. I doubt we'll get the same consideration from the OKC cops."

Cass wanted to kiss him again but didn't. Cameras of

every sort were aimed in their direction and had been re-
cording every moment of the confrontation. She turned and
raised her hand. "Move 'em out!"

The outriders pushed the herd slowly, and like a lum-
bering black wave, the cattle shuffled forward. The cruisers moved out of the way, and the deputies turned to crowd
control to keep zealous onlookers safe. The herd lined out,
and the trail drive continued. As the lead riders neared the
flood plain leading to Lake Overholser, Cass doubled back
to check with each rider.

"We'll take them around the lake road to the spillway
and down the riverbed. It's mostly dry. We can cross under
I-40 that way."

The herd moved without incident. A Bethany police car
led the way while other units shut down intersections to
traffic so they could pass safely. The lead cows balked at
the dip down the riverbank, but the smell of water over-
came their fear. They plunged over, and the rest of the herd
followed. The riders allowed the cattle to drink their fill
and then pushed them down the wide, sandy river bottom.

The sun climbed overhead, passed zenith, and the herd
kept moving. They needed to find a place to move the cattle out of the riverbed and back up to a surface street. Cord
and Chance rode ahead to find a spot and a few minutes
later, Cord galloped back. He joined Cass, and the expression on his face left her worried.

"Chance is talking to the Oklahoma City cops. They
say we can't use Fifteenth Street to push the herd through."

"What? How the hell are we going to get them across
I-44 then? We can't swim them down the river, and the first
dam is just past Meridian. If we don't push them out of the
river soon, we'll be stuck."

"Duh. Chance is negotiating with them. I'm thinking we
take them just past MacArthur. They're dredging the river
there, and it's a construction zone. We can drive the herd

to the start of the riverside park and use the bike and running trail. That gets us under I-44. If we go all the way to
Agnew, we can take them straight under the Stockyard City
arch and to the stockyard pens. With the publicity you're
getting, all the merchants are lined up ready to help." He
held up his cell phone. "My contact at the chamber of com-
merce says they're ready to block the intersections with
their private vehicles if that's what it takes." He passed the
phone to her so she could read the text for herself.

"I...this is just crazy."

"And?"

She laughed. Cord seemed convinced they could do this.
And Chance was a white knight fighting battles for her. "I
say we unleash some crazy."

They managed a steady speed of almost two miles an
hour. Chance hadn't returned, and she hoped he hadn't been
arrested. Cord assured her his brother wouldn't let that happen, but she noticed he looked worried and checked both
his phone and the view downriver every few minutes for
some sign of Chance.

When the herd reached the construction area, the lead
riders turned up the gently sloping bank. Cass topped out
and reined in her horse. A cluster of police cars, with lights
flashing, lined up to block any sort of egress to the street.
She was relieved to find Chance, dismounted and talking
to a policeman. Chance waved his hands to make some
point and while she couldn't hear his words, his posture
and every gesture indicated how angry and frustrated he
was. The cop responded with a jutted chin and hands stiff
at his side as if he had to keep them there with effort.

She waved her riders and the herd on to the east. They
wouldn't try the street, instead opting for Cord's suggestion.
They would follow the upper riverbank, crossing under the
roads between them and the stockyards. There was only un-
developed land until they hit Meridian Avenue. Any prob-

lem would likely crop up once they hit the bike trails and developed area between there and the stockyards where the land narrowed.

Cass couldn't help but glance over her shoulder to keep an eye on Chance. And then all hell broke loose. Staccato pop-pop-pops sounded like gunfire. Her horse reared. The cattle panicked and surged every which way. She struggled to stay in the saddle as cops drew their weapons. Chance yelled and shoved the cop he'd been talking to out of the way as a knot of cows stampeded in their direction. He managed to hang on to his horse's reins, leaped up on the animal and rode into the melee.

She heard Buddy barking wildly as he darted this way and that, nipping at the heels of the cattle, herding them away from the street. Two steers darted past the police line headed for a cluster of onlookers. She kicked her sorrel into a gallop to head them off. Buddy raced past her, nothing but a gray blur. Then everything went into slow motion.

A police car swerved in front of the cows to stop them. The driver slammed on his brakes when he realized he was going to hit them, and he twisted the wheel. The car went into a slide, the tires screaming in protest. Cass's horrified yell was lost in the confusion. Buddy, intent on the steers, never saw the car. Despite all the yelling, the sirens, the mooing of panicked cattle, she still heard the sickening thud of metal meeting flesh and bone. Buddy yelped as he went flying. Forgetting everything but her dog, she jumped down and ran to the injured animal.

"Oh, Buddy, Buddy, Buddy." She sobbed, tears streaming unchecked down her cheeks, leaving red streaks in the dust coating her skin. "Easy, boy. Easy. Just lie still. It's going to be okay. Oh, please, God, let him be okay." She touched his head, and he licked her wrist.

A warm hand gripped her shoulder with gentle fingers.

"We'll get him to the vet's, Cass." Chance's voice cracked but he cleared his throat. "Heidi! Get a blanket!"

Cass didn't hear Heidi's reply but moments later, the woman appeared, her stylish heels sinking into the red Oklahoma dirt. She dropped to her knees, unheedful of her stockings and tailored linen skirt. The woman clutched a baseball-print fleece blanket and spread it out next to Buddy.

While Cass stroked the dog's head and crooned to him, Chance carefully checked for injuries. With the gentleness of a father handling a newborn baby, he lifted Buddy just enough so that Heidi could slip the blanket beneath him. The dog whined but didn't move. A police officer appeared, and before Cass could tell him off, he picked up one edge of the blanket.

"My car is this way, Mr. Barron. I'll take the dog to the emergency vet's."

"I'm going, too." She stood up and bent to take a corner of the blanket.

Chance pulled her against his chest. "No, love. You can't. You need to get the herd back together and get them to the stockyards. Cord will help. I'll go with Buddy. I promise he'll be okay. I won't let Buddy out of my sight." His arms tightened around her, and he kissed the top of her head. The only way to beat the old man was for her to lead a triumphant parade into the stockyards. She had to do this. For herself. And for the two of them. "Now go do what you have to do. You have to finish this."

He cupped her cheeks as she tilted her face up, and he dipped his head to kiss her. His thumbs caressed her skin, smearing tears and dirt. "Cowgirls don't cry, Cass. And you are the finest damn cowgirl I've ever had the honor to meet. Now get your pretty ass back in that saddle and ride. Do this for you. For your dad. For the Crazy M Ranch." *For us,* he added silently.

Cass drew in a long, shuddering breath. Her chin came up even as she leaned her forehead against Chance's very solid chest. "Take care of Buddy, Chance. I'll see you on the other side."

She stepped back, but he didn't release her. Not yet. Not until he claimed her mouth again. She clung to him through the kiss and for a moment longer. As his arms fell away, she turned on her heel and strode into the middle of the chaos, her back straight, her head held high.

Red waited nearby, one front foot stuck in the loop of the reins. He stood still as she approached and freed his foot. Grabbing up the reins, she shoved her boot in the stirrup, mounted and settled into her saddle. In less time than she anticipated, all the cattle were rounded up. Several of her riders had been injured, two seriously. A few of the cops suffered cuts and bruises but they were all on their feet. Cass was down to a handful of drovers, the herd was skittish, and they still had just over three miles to go.

One of the cops yelled and waved to her. She recognized him as the man Chance had been speaking with, so she waited as he approached. He grabbed one rein and stared up at her.

"Firecrackers. Some idiot let loose with a package of Black Cats." The cop shook his head and spit on the ground. He glanced around and winced at the scene. "Keep to the riverbank and the park. We'll patrol the overpasses, Miss Morgan. No one else will disrupt your trail drive. I didn't want it to come to this, that's for sure. But I had orders, ma'am." As they watched, one of her riders was loaded into the back of an ambulance. "No sirree, I sure didn't want it to come to this."

"Neither did I."

"Good luck, Miss Morgan." He turned loose of her horse and stepped back as she put her heels to the sorrel.

Someone called her name, and she glanced back. A bevy

of reporters clamored for her attention but she ignored them. The squad car with Chance and Buddy had already disappeared. The ambulance with her drover also pulled away, lights flashing, though the driver waited until the vehicle was well past the cattle herd before the sirens blared.

With the herd back in some semblance of order, she returned to work. She would finish this. Come hell or high water, she'd get these cattle to the sale and get the money she needed to pay off the mortgage. Cyrus Barron damn sure wasn't getting her ranch. For a brief moment, she wondered what the man would do when he discovered two of his sons had defected to her side in this private war of theirs.

Cord trotted up beside her and handed her a wet bandanna. "You might want to give your face a swipe, especially before we hit Stockyard City. At the moment, you look like you've been ridden hard and put up wet."

"Gee, Cord. I bet the girls just swoon when you give them a compliment."

He laughed. "I like you, Cassidy Morgan. Too bad my little brother met you first."

She wiped her face and winced when she saw the dirty streaks staining the bandanna. "When this is done, I'm going to stand in the shower until there's no hot water left in the tank."

"I'd offer to scrub your back, but I have the feeling Chance will volunteer first."

Up ahead, a cow broke ranks and before she could react, Cord urged his horse forward and charged after the miscreant steer. She watched the expert way he worked. Chance sat a horse just as well. And he'd helped her restring barbed wire fence like he'd done it all his life. Neither of these men acted as she expected. The Barrons were the closest thing to royalty in Oklahoma—in fact, one media wag had dubbed them Red Dirt Royalty. One brother was a US Senator. Another presided over a media empire that included newspapers, TV stations, resorts and an amusement park. A Barron and the senior partner in his own law firm, Chance hobnobbed with the rich and powerful.

But when he came to her place, when he wore his jeans and work shirt like he was born to them, Chance became a different man. He sat on the porch with her, holding her hand and petting Buddy...

At the thought of the beloved dog, her chest threatened to cave in. Buddy had to be okay. Chance would take care of him.

A steer ambled away from the herd, and she shook her head. This was no time to be daydreaming—especially about a man like Chance Barron declaring his love for her. "Yaw," she yelled at the cow, urging Red after the critter.

The herd passed under Meridian without incident. Even though the riverside park system began here, there was little open space behind the hotels and office complexes. Land between "civilization" and the river narrowed. Her riders strung out in a thin line. The next hurdle would be Portland Avenue and then the I-44/I-40 interchange. She shuddered at the thought of any of the cattle making it up onto the interstate highway. Two miles. Two miles to the stockyards. She needed things to stay quiet for two more miles. She managed a deep breath. Chance was right. She would succeed.

She continuously rode back and forth, encouraging her drovers, chasing steers back into line and trying not to get her hopes up. They passed Portland Avenue. Just as with the Meridian corridor, a large police presence kept traffic and onlookers at bay. A couple of the officers even offered sur-reptitious thumbs-up gestures as she passed beneath them.

The strip of land they traversed widened, and the herd bunched up a little more. Ahead, an office building and huge parking lot would choke them down into almost single file. Red whickered and shook his head. His lathered neck proved how hard he'd been working. All the horses, and their riders, too, looked worn out.

Boots, still riding at the head of the herd, let out a whoop. She stood in her stirrups to see what new problem they faced. To her surprise, a knot of riders advanced from the east. Clicking her tongue, she eased Red into a trot and headed to meet them. She reined in as she reached Boots and let the riders approach.

The lead rider stopped and tipped his hat. "Miz Morgan? We're members of the Stockyard City Sheriff's Posse."

She cringed. What now? She thought the sheriff's department had accepted Chance's injunction. Before she could respond, he continued.

"We heard about that dust up back down the way. We'd have been here sooner to help but some of us needed to go get our horses."

She blinked and then blinked again. "Help? You're here to help?"

"Yes, ma'am, we are. Some of these boys might look like city slickers, but we know how to ride and work cattle." Since the man wore dress pants and a button-down shirt with a loosened tie, he likely qualified as one of those city slickers.

Her eyes burned, and she blinked hard. "Help." She glanced at Boots and answered his big grin with one of her own. She finally remembered her manners. "Uh…thanks!"

The ten riders headed west and circled around to fill in blank spots along the herd. She twisted in her saddle so she could watch, and relaxed after a few minutes. Yeah, even though that one guy probably left his suit coat in his office, he sat his horse with ease. Beside her, Boots grinned like the Cheshire cat.

"What?"

He laughed. "If you could see the expression on your

face, sugar. You look like you just walked into a glass door, thinking it was open."

"Gee, thanks, Uncle Boots. But...yeah. I guess the description fits. I feel like I've been sucker punched. I...I just can't believe all these people want to help. The media. The cops." Another word hovered on the tip of her tongue, but she didn't voice it.

"Chance."

Yeah. That was the one. "He's a Barron, Uncle Boots. His father is the cause of all of this. I—" She huffed out a breath. "How can I trust him?"

They rode in silence for a few minutes before Boots spoke up. "Look inside his heart, baby girl. Tally up all the things he's done to help you. Despite his father. Sometimes blood is thicker than just about anything. But sometimes, a woman loves a man so much she's willing to give up everything for him because she knows he loves her more than anything in the world."

She glanced at him. "That sounds like you're talking about Momma and Daddy."

"I suppose I am, Cassie. Even way back then, Cyrus Barron was a man on the way up. He had a big ranch with lots of cattle, and the horses he bred were some of the finest in the country. He didn't lease his oil and gas royalty rights. He started his own drilling company. And that eventually became Barron Oil. If your momma had married him, she'd have been a rich woman."

Boots took off his hat and wiped his forehead with a bandanna before continuing. "Your daddy was a rodeo cowboy without a pot to piss in. But after that beating, layin' there in the hospital, your momma holdin' his hand and tellin' him how much she loved him, he figured he'd better do something with his life. He scraped together every bit of cash and credit he had and bought the home place. He knew rodeo. And he knew rodeo stock. He started small, but the rodeo folks knew they'd get quality if they hired him. Your momma was there each step of the way, keepin' the books, cleanin' out pens, whatever it took. Until she got sick."

Cass nodded and swallowed hard against the nausea. Her mother had been so sick from pneumonia and despite the breathing tubes and everything else, she couldn't fight the disease.

"You find a love like what your momma and daddy shared, baby girl, you grab on with both hands and never let go." He dipped his chin and stared forward. "Highway's just up a ways. We'd better get ready."

Cass reined Red to a stop on the slope leading up to the interstate right-of-way. A line of riders flanked the road on each side of the overpass. To her now-practiced eye, the herd looked as worn out as her drovers and their horses. Just about a mile now. She exhaled in relief when the last drag rider passed by and disappeared under the overpass. She followed.

On the other side, the herd had bunched tightly again and moved forward like some weird amoeba. Cass could only imagine what the scene looked like from above. Maybe someday, she'd catch a news report to see the footage shot from a helicopter. In the meantime, she had cows to get to market. She rode up the line, urging tired riders and cattle onward.

The news helicopter disappeared, heading west. Cass glanced over her shoulder hoping it wasn't focusing on something bad happening to the drag riders. It kept flying straight and as she watched, lightning flickered in the clouds massing on the western horizon.

"I knew it," she muttered. "Red skies in the morning, sailors…and cowboys take warning." She glanced at her watch. With luck, she'd have the herd delivered to the stockyards, and they'd all be safely in their pens by the time the storm moved in. Nothing to panic over. Yet.

Seventeen

The new bridge with the fancy streetlights loomed ahead. Agnew Avenue. If Chance was right, the street would be blocked to traffic, and she could bring the herd right down the middle of the street. Cord cantered up to her and slowed his horse to match hers.

"About time for you to move up, Cass. You should be at the head of this parade."

She shook her head. "I didn't do this for attention, Cord. If your father had stayed out of things, I'd be back on the ranch with the loan paid." She felt her face flush as her blood pressure spiked.

"Yeah, he's a real sonofabitch. And I figure he's probably not quite done yet. Chance will do everything he can to stop whatever the old man has up his sleeve."

"But…?"

"But?"

"Yeah, I heard a *but* on the end of that sentence." She turned to stare at him, and more than her blood pressure hammered in her ears. "He's going to turn Chance against me, isn't he?" She muttered a string of cusswords but didn't smile when Cord laughed at her. "Damn the man!"

"Which one?"

His quiet question surprised her. "Your…" She blinked and shut her mouth while she considered her answer, which came in the form of a question. "Will he succeed?"

Cord wouldn't look at her, but his shoulders rose in what might be a negligent shrug. "Yesterday, I would have said yeah. The old man always gets what he wants. But today? I don't know." He reined his horse around and headed toward the rear of the herd before she could reply.

She touched spurs to Red's sides, and the big horse quickened his pace. If Cyrus Barron was waiting to stop her at the end of this, by golly she'd be front and center to confront him.

Boots glanced at her as she joined him. "About time you got up here."

She laughed, but it sounded mirthless. "How did this get so out of control, Uncle Boots?"

"People, honey. People always complicate matters. But we're almost there."

Their horses' hooves clopped on the asphalt as they stepped off the curb. Sheriff's cruisers had the street blocked at the off ramp from I-40, and the way was clear to the south. Almost as if sensing the end was near, horses and cattle all picked up the pace. The gateway arch stretched above the street ahead of them. A cowboy on horseback and a long-horned steer bracketed the words "Stockyard City" displayed across the metal span. As she passed beneath it, Cass breathed again. This was it. They'd done it. People lined the street while cameras—digital, phone and video—all preserved the moment for posterity.

"Cass!"

She glanced over in the direction the voice came from. Chance! He stood on the bumper of a pickup truck waving at her. And then the sweetest sound in the world reached her ears—Buddy's excited barks. Her chest swelled with so much happiness she might burst wide open. Her grin spread from ear to ear. She probably looked like a complete idiot but didn't care.

Cord trotted up from behind her and rode past, tipping

the brim of his hat as he went by. He stopped in front of Chance and dismounted. The brothers exchanged places, Chance mounting the horse, and Cord taking charge of Buddy. The men shook hands. Cord said something Cass couldn't hear, but it must have been about her because Chance turned to look at her. Then he smiled, and nothing else mattered.

Police and the fire department had Exchange Boulevard to the east and Agnew to the south blocked off. The cattle had no place to go but turn right and head straight to the National Stockyards. Cheering people lined both sides of the street and surprisingly, the cattle didn't seem bothered by all the hoopla. Cass tamped down her excitement. Until those steers were penned, went through the auction tomorrow morning and she had a check to give Cyrus Barron, she couldn't celebrate.

Chance risked a quick touch on her arm as he rode knee to knee with her. Buddy woofed and wagged his tail, his head hanging out of the pickup truck window as Cord carefully drove by them.

"The pup had some bruised ribs, and his right hip is tender where he landed on it. The vet says as long as Buddy takes it easy, he'll be fine."

She inhaled and blew out a little puff of air. "Thank you."

He glanced at her. "For what?"

"For everything. For taking care of Buddy. For helping despite everything…" Her voice trailed off and left hanging just what that *everything* comprised. In her head, she finished the thought—despite her mistrust, her anger, her accusations.

"You had every right, Cass. I wasn't completely honest with you. And I'm truly sorry for that. I won't lie to you again. Not ever."

She flashed him a cocky grin. "Can I have that in writing and notarized, Mr. Lawyer Guy?"

He chuckled but choked off the sound as he stared at the knot of people waiting ahead. A beefy man in Western clothes, his sleeves rolled up to reveal brawny forearms, his hat pushed back off his forehead, argued vehemently with a tall, distinguished man wearing a tailored suit that cost more than many people made in a month.

Damn. The old man was back from Vegas. He glanced at Cass and offered her a smile. Things were going to get ugly in a heartbeat.

"Are you going to tell me everything will be all right?"

"No."

"Good. So what *are* you going to tell me?"

"That's my father up there. I suspect the other man is the sales manager of the stockyards. If the old man stays true to form, he's threatening all sorts of dire consequences about now."

"Then we'd better go face whatever those consequences are." She clucked to her horse and trotted forward.

Chance followed at a jog. Cord had parked nearby and Buddy was there, hackles raised, ears back. He could almost feel the growl forming in the dog's chest as he reined to a stop next to Cassie.

"I don't give a damn, Mr. Barron. The last time I looked, your name wasn't on the bottom of my paycheck. You can scream and cuss all you want but since you don't own this place, I'm not about to turn away any cattle brought here for sale."

Camera crews homed in on the altercation, and Chance winced. The family would need a lot of damage control after the news tonight. The old man, red in the face and sputtering, jabbed his finger in the man's chest.

"I will own this miserable excuse for a sale barn, and I will fire your insolent ass. I will shut this place down and fire everyone even remotely associated with the stockyards. Do you understand me?"

Cyrus Barron straightened to his full height and looked for all the world like some old revival preacher raining fire and brimstone on his congregation. No one had called his bluff in ages. He pulled out his phone, called his assistant and snarled terse instructions Chance didn't hear but could imagine. With a cold, calculating smile, Cyrus faced the sales manager, ignoring Cass and Chance. The standoff lasted what felt like an hour but was ten minutes in reality. The herd bunched up in the street, and people waited breathlessly.

The manager's cell phone rang. He answered, his face draining of color as he listened. He stammered and hemmed but in the end, he ducked his head and mumbled something. Turning on his heel, he walked back to his wranglers and told them to shut the gates and go home. The stockyards had closed for the day.

The old man turned his cold smile on Cass, and adrenaline surged through Chance's body, leaving his fingers and toes tingling and burning.

"I'm disappointed in you."

Chance straightened his shoulders as the old man focused on him. He was pretty sure the smirk he plastered on his face was a mirror image of the one his father wore. "Makes two of us. This has gone far enough, Cyrus."

"Indeed it has. I've already instructed my attorneys to remove you from the trust."

Cass gasped but he ignored her. If he broke eye contact now, the old man would think he'd won, and Chance wasn't about to let that happen. His expression didn't change. "It will be an interesting court battle, considering I'm the one who drew up the trust papers in the first place. Did you ever read them, Cyrus? Or did you just sign them?"

There. There was the flicker in the old man's eyes he'd been waiting for. He'd learned the art of confrontation from the master himself. He quirked one corner of his mouth.

"Oh, I forgot rule number one. If you can't trust family, you can't trust family. You should have remembered that one, Cyrus."

"It's too late for your little who—"

Lightning fast, his fists wrapped in the lapels of his father's suit. "Don't go there, Old Man. You say what's on the tip of your tongue, I'll happily spend the night in jail for knocking the crap out of you."

Cyrus glared but didn't finish the sentence. "It's still too late, *son.* She can't make the balloon payment on that loan unless she sells those steers by five o'clock tomorrow afternoon. And that will not happen."

"Yes, it will. I'll buy the cattle from her."

Chance and his father whipped their heads around at the new voice. The crowd grew silent as anticipation filled the air. The newcomer ignored Cyrus and walked over to Cass, where she'd remained mounted.

"Miss Morgan, I'm J. Rand Davis."

As his gaze darted between the man and Cass, Chance had to stifle a laugh. If there was a man Cyrus Barron hated even more than Ben Morgan, it had to be Joseph Randolph Davis. They'd been rival wildcatters back in the early days of the oil boom; now both of them were among the richest men in the country.

Cass dismounted and offered her hand. "Mr. Davis, I suspect it's going to be my pleasure to meet you."

"I certainly hope so." He glanced at his smartphone, checked a couple of screens then smiled at her. "According to the closing spot prices on the Chicago Commodities Exchange, prime grass-fed Black Angus cattle are going for a hundred and forty-seven."

Chance did a quick mental calculation. The price was per hundredweight and given the size and quality of Cass's steers, she'd make over five hundred thousand dollars. Cass looked stunned as she also did the math.

"I have trucks lined up, and we'll get a final weight on 'em but I'm prepared to hand you a certified check for three hundred thousand dollars as a down payment. Once the weigh-in is final, I will cut another check for the remainder."

Cass glanced over at Chance, her eyes wide with surprise. It was enough to pay off the note. He nodded to her. "It's a fair price, Cass. And I figure Mr. Davis is good for the rest."

She offered her hand, and Davis shook it. He handed over a check and she glanced at it, stared for a long moment, blinked and barely resisted doing a happy dance right there in the middle of the street.

Davis spoke up immediately. "Knowing Cyrus like I do, I didn't want to take any chances that he'd wiggle out of the deal." He reached for the inside breast pocket of his sport coat and pulled out some folded papers. "Here's the bill of sale with the terms and deadline for payment of the additional funds"

Cass accepted them and with a confused expression, glanced over at Chance. "Will you look it over?"

He took the papers and unfolded them as Davis added, "Look it over, Chancellor. If Miss Baxter agrees, she can sign it and we'll start loading these steers."

Chance read through them, his practiced eye picking out the important parts. Everything was just as Mr. Davis had outlined. He handed the sheaf of papers back to Cass as Davis passed his pen to her. She took the time to read every page, and Chance couldn't help the grin forming. She glanced at him finally and he nodded. She signed, using his back.

Chance had almost forgotten about his father until the old man snorted. "You wait, Rand Davis. You think you've won this time, but I guarantee this thing isn't over between us." Then he turned a baleful stare on Chance. "As for you, I'll deal with you later."

Davis offered a frosty smile. "Careful what you threaten, Cyrus."

The old man spun around and stomped off to his chauffeured Lincoln. In a matter of minutes, the stockyard wranglers reappeared, opened the gates to some loading pens, and the herd was moved off the street. A spontaneous celebration erupted behind them, but Chance and Cass remained with Mr. Davis, watching as the cattle were transferred up the chutes and loaded into the waiting trucks.

Chance watched one of the richest oilmen in the world chat with the woman he loved. Three months ago, on that snowy Chicago night, he would never have guessed he'd be standing on a dusty street in Stockyard City watching this scene.

But then, all of a sudden, Davis clamped his mouth shut in the middle of a sentence, and his eyes narrowed in anger. Chance turned around, thinking his father had returned.

To his surprise, Cord stood there like a deer caught in headlights. The two men stared at each other, and Chance couldn't help but compare the standoff to a scene from a Western movie—the gunfighters on Main Street, fingers flexing over the handles of their six-shooters, each waiting for the other to make a move. He'd never seen his brother look so unnerved.

After a long, tense moment, Davis turned his head and focused his attention on Cassie. "I'll have the certified check for the rest of the money delivered to you tomorrow, Miss Morgan."

She offered her hand again, after wiping it down her thigh. As dusty as her jeans appeared, she probably didn't clean much dirt off, but she made the effort. "Thank you again, Mr. Davis. I…" On impulse, she raised up on her toes and planted a quick kiss on his cheek. "I couldn't have done this without you."

Davis shook his head and glanced toward Chance. "No, honey. I think you had all the help you needed right there at your side." He offered his hand to Chance. "You take care of this little lady."

Chance shook hands with Rand. "I will, sir." He slipped his arm around Cassie's shoulders and hugged her closer to his side. "You did it, darlin'."

She smiled up at him. "No. *We* did it. I'm sorry I ever doubted you."

He shook his head. "Don't apologize. To be honest, I wasn't sure I could stand up to the old man. But you made me want to. Your belief in me, Cass. That's what gave me the courage."

He caught movement in the corner of his eye and turned just in time to see Davis stop in front of Cord. The two men exchanged what appeared to be heated words until Chance realized something was off about Cord's posture. His shoulders drooped a little, and while he hadn't bowed his head, he wasn't quite looking Mr. Davis in the eye, either.

"Now what the hell is that all about?"

Cass leaned around him to watch. "I…wow. Cord almost looks cowed. He's definitely on the defensive."

Davis walked away but Cord stood rooted to the spot. Chance wrapped his fingers around Cassie's hand and tugged her with him as he approached his brother. "Cord?"

"Don't."

"Don't what? What's going on?"

"Nothing."

"That didn't look like nothing to me."

"Leave it be, Chance. It's…"

Cass squeezed his arm before he could speak again. "Not now, Chance."

Cord flashed her an appreciative look then turned on

a high-wattage smile. Chance knew that look. Cord had dodged some sort of bullet, but that was okay. He'd eventually pin down his brother to find out what that discussion had been about.

The stockyards manager approached and cleared his throat. "Sorry to interrupt, folks, but the last cow has been loaded. Five hundred on the nose, Miss Morgan. Mr. Davis already paid the loading fees. If you'll just sign this receipt, we're all done." He thrust a battered aluminum clipboard in her direction, and she scribbled her name across the bottom. The man made a show of tearing off the receipt and handed it to her with a flourish.

"Congratulations, ma'am. We were all rooting for you."

Chance glanced at her upturned face, and his heart lurched. Damn but he loved this woman. "You did it, Cass. I am so freaking proud of you, I'm about to bust. I love you, darlin', with everything I am."

Cord punched him on the arm. "Well, don't just stand there, little brother. Kiss the girl."

Epilogue

Cass adjusted the blue garter on her thigh then slipped her foot into the Justin Western boot. She flounced the full skirt of her wedding dress and turned around. Her maid of honor and two bridesmaids had crystal champagne flutes in their hands ready to toast her nuptials. She glanced at the other person in the room. Boots had a finger stuck between his buttoned-up collar and his neck, trying to stretch the shirt. With a knowing smile, she adjusted his silver-and-black bolo tie. "As soon as you walk me down the aisle, Uncle Boots, you can unbutton. Promise."

The old man muttered something under his breath, and she had to bite back her giggle. She felt giddy, her thoughts scattered as her nerves thrummed in anticipation.

After selling the herd, Chance had handed over the deed to the Crazy M, admitting he'd already paid off the loan. She'd insisted on paying him back and did so five minutes before he dropped to a knee and asked her to marry him.

She smiled at the memory.

She squelched the one niggling thought that she was about to make the worst mistake of her life. She must be insane to join Cyrus Barron's family by her own free will. But if she was crazy, she didn't care.

"Answer me one thing, baby girl."

She shook the negative thoughts from her mind and focused on Boots. "Yes?"

"Would your life be better without him?"

A nervous laugh burbled up before she could catch it. "What? Are you reading my mind now?"

"Be honest, Cassidy Anne. With me, but most important with yourself. If you walked away now, would you look back in relief or regret?"

She stared out the window. Knots of people gathered on the lawn in front of the chapel. She glimpsed what looked like a rugby scrum—the Barron brothers. They'd all come to support Chance, and each one of them had privately offered her friendship and brotherhood. She couldn't breathe for a minute, and her vision fogged. When it cleared, she saw only Chance standing there surrounded by his family. Business-wise, he'd put his foot down. His law firm was his and not part of Barron Enterprises, though he continued to represent the family's various entities. Chance had talked things through with her before he agreed to remain as the Barron's legal counsel. He glanced toward the window almost as if he knew she watched.

"That answers my question."

Startled from her reverie she turned to stare at Boots. "What? I didn't say anything."

"You didn't have to, Cassie. The smile on your face said it all. Now let's get this rodeo goin' before I strangle in this monkey suit."

Chance stood at the front of the church looking outwardly calm, but he felt as if he was on a sinking life raft in a raging storm. Cord stood on his left, along with his other brothers. Heidi and her husband occupied the front pew of the small chapel, along with the caretaker couple who'd practically raised the brothers, Beth and John Sanders. Cyrus Barron hadn't bothered to attend, not that he was surprised. The rest of his family stood up for him, though, and that's all that mattered.

The front doors opened, and the congregation hushed. An ancient organ wheezed out music vaguely resembling something classical. Two bridesmaids and the maid of honor floated down the aisle. He squinted against the bright sun backlighting the door and made out Boots's stocky form. As the man stepped into the more sedate light of the nave, with Cass on his arm, Chance held his breath.

She looked beautiful. Absolutely, totally, completely stunning. His heart galloped then smoothed out its rhythm. Her gaze held his and any sense of foreboding dissipated. God, but he loved this woman with every ounce of his being. The feeling of rightness overwhelmed him, and he blinked away the sudden moisture gathering in his eyes.

Cass stopped in front of him, leaned up on her tiptoes and kissed his cheek. "Hey, don't you know cowboys aren't supposed to cry?"

He smiled and whispered. "I heard it was cowgirls never cry, they just get back on and ride." Yes, Chance Barron always knew exactly what he wanted. And he always got it.

* * * * *

*Don't miss
the next book in Silver James's*
RED DIRT ROYALTY *series*
THE COWGIRL'S LITTLE SECRET
*Available April 2015
From Silver James and Harlequin Desire!*

COMING NEXT MONTH FROM

HARLEQUIN

Desire

Available February 3, 2015

#2353 HER FORBIDDEN COWBOY
Moonlight Beach Bachelors • by Charlene Sands
When his late wife's younger sister needs a place to heal after being jilted at the altar, country-and-western star Zane Williams offers comfort at his beachfront mansion. But when he takes her in his arms, they enter forbidden territory...

#2354 HIS LOST AND FOUND FAMILY
Texas Cattleman's Club: After the Storm
by Sarah M. Anderson
Tracking down his estranged wife to their hometown hospital, entrepreneur Jake Holt discovers she's lost her memory—and had his baby. Will their renewed love stand the test when she remembers what drove them apart?

#2355 THE BLACKSTONE HEIR
Billionaires and Babies • by Dani Wade
Mill owner Jacob Blackstone is all business; bartender KC Gatlin goes with the flow. But her baby secret is about to shake things up as these two very different people come together for their child's future...and their own.

#2356 THIRTY DAYS TO WIN HIS WIFE
Brides and Belles • by Andrea Laurence
Thinking twice after a reckless Vegas elopement, two best friends find their divorce plans derailed by a surprise pregnancy. Will a relationship trial run prove they might be perfect partners, after all?

#2357 THE TEXAN'S ROYAL M.D.
Duchess Diaries • by Merline Lovelace
When a sexy doctor from a royal bloodline saves the nephew of a Texas billionaire, she loses her heart in the process. But secrets from her past may keep her from the man she loves...

#2358 TERMS OF A TEXAS MARRIAGE
by Lauren Canan
The fine print of a hundred-year-old land lease will dictate Shea Hardin's fate: she must marry a bully or lose it all. But what happens when she falls for her fake husband...hard?

YOU CAN FIND MORE INFORMATION ON UPCOMING HARLEQUIN® TITLES, FREE EXCERPTS AND MORE AT WWW.HARLEQUIN.COM.

HDCNM0115

REQUEST YOUR FREE BOOKS!
2 FREE NOVELS PLUS 2 FREE GIFTS!

♦HARLEQUIN®

Desire

ALWAYS POWERFUL, PASSIONATE AND PROVOCATIVE

YES! Please send me 2 FREE Harlequin Desire® novels and my 2 FREE gifts (gifts are worth about $10). After receiving them, if I don't wish to receive any more books, I can return the shipping statement marked "cancel." If I don't cancel, I will receive 6 brand-new novels every month and be billed just $4.55 per book in the U.S. or $4.99 per book in Canada. That's a savings of at least 13% off the cover price! It's quite a bargain! Shipping and handling is just 50¢ per book in the U.S. and 75¢ per book in Canada.* I understand that accepting the 2 free books and gifts places me under no obligation to buy anything. I can always return a shipment and cancel at any time. Even if I never buy another book, the two free books and gifts are mine to keep forever.

225/326 HDN F4ZC

Name _____ (PLEASE PRINT) _____

Address _____ Apt. #

City _____ State/Prov. _____ Zip/Postal Code

Signature (if under 18, a parent or guardian must sign)

Mail to the **Harlequin® Reader Service:**

IN U.S.A.: P.O. Box 1867, Buffalo, NY 14240-1867
IN CANADA: P.O. Box 609, Fort Erie, Ontario L2A 5X3

Want to try two free books from another line?
Call 1-800-873-8635 or visit www.ReaderService.com

* Terms and prices subject to change without notice. Prices do not include applicable taxes. Sales tax applicable in N.Y. Canadian residents will be charged applicable taxes. Offer not valid in Quebec. This offer is limited to one order per household. Not valid for current subscribers to Harlequin Desire books. All orders subject to credit approval. Credit or debit balances in a customer's account(s) may be offset by any other outstanding balance owed by or to the customer. Please allow 4 to 6 weeks for delivery. Offer available while quantities last.

Your Privacy—The Harlequin® Reader Service is committed to protecting your privacy. Our Privacy Policy is available online at www.ReaderService.com or upon request from the Harlequin Reader Service.

We make a portion of our mailing list available to reputable third parties that offer products we believe may interest you. If you prefer that we not exchange your name with third parties, or if you wish to clarify or modify your communication preferences, please visit us at www.ReaderService.com/consumerchoice or write to us at Harlequin Reader Service Preference Service, P.O. Box 9062, Buffalo, NY 14269. Include your complete name and address.

HD13R

SPECIAL EXCERPT FROM

Here's a sneak peek at the next
TEXAS CATTLEMAN'S CLUB:
AFTER THE STORM *installment,*
HIS LOST AND FOUND FAMILY
by *Sarah M. Anderson*

Separated and on the verge of divorce, Jake Holt is determined to confront his wife. But when he arrives in Royal, Texas, he finds that Skye has been keeping secrets...

Jake had spent the past four years pointedly not caring about what his family was doing. They'd wanted him to put the family above his wife. Nothing had been more important to him than Skye.

He was not staying in Royal long. Just enough to get Skye back on her feet and figure out where they stood.

Just then, the baby made a little hiccup-sigh noise that pulled at his heartstrings.

Jake's brother picked the baby up so smoothly that Jake was jealous.

"Grace, honey—this is your daddy," Keaton said as he rubbed her back. Then, to Jake, he added, "You ready?"

Not really—but Jake wasn't going to admit that to Keaton. He tried to cradle his arms in the right way. Then Keaton laid the baby in them.

The world seemed to tilt off its axis as Jake looked down into his daughter's eyes. They were a pale blue—

just like her mother's. Up close now, he could see that Grace had wispy hairs on her head that were so white and fine they were almost see-through.

She didn't start bawling, which he took as a good sign. Instead, she waved her tiny hands around, so of course he had to offer her one of his fingers. When she latched on to it, he felt lost and yet *not* lost at the same time.

He was responsible for this little girl from this moment until the day he drew his last breath. The weight of it hit him so hard that if he hadn't already been sitting, his knees would have buckled.

This was his daughter. He and Skye had created this little person.

God, he wished Skye was here with him. That things between them had been different. That he'd been different.

But he couldn't change the past, not when his present—and his future—was gripping his little finger with surprising strength.

Don't miss what happens next in
HIS LOST AND FOUND FAMILY
by Sarah M. Anderson!

Available February 2015,
wherever Harlequin® Desire books and ebooks are sold.